Daniil Rozental has a diverse background and a profound passion for writing. Born in Moscow, he spent his formative years in Washington DC studying international relations at the American University and Georgetown University, graduating with distinction.

Following his studies, Daniil embarked on a journey to Paris, where he seamlessly merged his entrepreneurial spirit with love for literature. While thriving as a successful businessman, his heart has always been dedicated to the art of writing. Throughout his career, Daniil contributed articles to numerous magazines. His latest literary publications are in the Russian-language anti-war almanac, *"Needle"*.

For Anna, who always believed in me.

Daniil Rozental

THE ZEROTH DAY

AUSTIN MACAULEY PUBLISHERS™

LONDON • CAMBRIDGE • NEW YORK • SHARJAH

A CIP catalogue record for this title is available from the British Library.

ISBN 9781035842490 (Paperback)
ISBN 9781035842506 (Hardback)
ISBN 9781035842520 (ePub e-book)
ISBN 9781035842513 (Audiobook)

www.austinmacauley.com

First Published 2024
Austin Macauley Publishers Ltd®
1 Canada Square
Canary Wharf
London
E14 5AA

To Mom and Dad for endless support; Kiril Adibekov for gentle guidance; Ksenya Rozdestvenskaya for helpful insights; Daniel Reneau for being the best friend; all friends who read and reread numerous drafts of the novel.
Illustrations by Nikita Chernoritskiy

1

The autumn was rainy. Succumbing to the heavy drops, yellowed leaves slipped from the trees and tumbled onto the wet pavement. Nature had shed its ochre corset, laying bare the innards of dacha plots as glimpsed through the ribs of their wooden fences—unevenly placed grey paving stones wending their way to dilapidated cottages, sagging sheds, and yard lights that had been switched off for a long while.

The fences, houses and even century-old pine trees seemed toylike against the huge wind turbine towering over the village. Although the giant white blades looming above the trees were not in motion, the windmill's drone muffled the rustling of the leaves and the pattering of the raindrops. The red warning lights flashing right below the clouds were barely legible, but their light would fill the night with a rhythmic flicker when darkness came.

The streets of the village were deserted. The infrequent pedestrians lowered their eyes when they met and hurriedly passed each other: they had to get home before sunset. In the evenings, the few residents who had stayed behind for the winter pulled their curtains shut. Sprawled on creaking couches, they would drink a cup of tea, clamp horn-like rubber antennae to their temples and, closing their eyes, dive into the Flow.

When the last candles were snuffed out, the village would be plunged into a darkness lacerated every few seconds by the flashes of red light. The first gust of wind gave impetus to the blades, which spun slowly at first, then ever more rapidly. The turbine's low, ear-piercing hum penetrated indoors, and none of the villagers could go outside without donning ear protectors. Fortunately, most of them had much earlier donned their horns (as they called them) and were voyaging in other worlds.

The village was practically bereft of nightlife except for Suren's Shop, a roadside store. Its proprietor (whose name, predictably, was Suren) had been awarded an electricity quota by some miracle (or by heftily bribing the right people, as the village scuttlebutt had it) and turned the shabby store into an epicurean oasis of pre-war life featuring bright lighting, cold beer, and frozen food.

Suren was in his forties. He sported a fresh white shirt and pressed black trousers and spoke with a thick Armenian accent. He had no employees, which was why he was rarely seen away from the store. That evening, he was polishing, as usual, the shop's preternaturally shiny counter, occasionally glancing at his reflection in a large mirror on the wall.

Opposite Suren stood a customer—Nikolai, a tall, broad-shouldered man in his fifties wearing classic fit jeans, a green checked flannel shirt and a brown raincoat. Stooping a little, the man stared at the floor, occasionally casting a beseeching glance at the merchant. The silent scene lasted for several seconds, before Suren, frowning, put down his rag and picked up a thick, plastic-covered notebook. After perusing his ledger, Suren closed the notebook and addressed the man.

"You have a debt of five thousand seven hundred and eighty-two rubles, my friend. You probably forgot. Write it down. I won't sell you anything until you pay me back."

Nikolai wanted to reply, but changing his mind and slouching even more abjectly, he turned on his heel and made for the exit.

"Your head!" Suren tried to warn him, but the man hit his head on the door jamb and left the store, cursing.

"Kolya, stop!" Suren shouted loudly after him.

Nikolai turned around and, nearly hitting his head a second time, walked back to the counter.

"When can you pay me back?" Suren asked, looking up at Nikolai.

"Soon, Suren. I've got a gig doing commercials coming up. I'll pay you back as soon as I get the money."

"You already promised." Suren shook his head. "You're not the only going through tough times. Times are tough for everyone."

"There is this one absolutely killer project. They said they would call," Nikolai lied, gazing at the floor.

"You said that before too," Suren grumbled. "Okay, what can I get you?"

Nikolai asked for some vegetables and a bottle of vodka. Handing him the bag of groceries, Suren nodded at a framed movie poster. It showed a man resembling Nikolai, only much younger. The man was kicking a chubby man armed with a pistol. The poster read: "*Fury of Light!* Nikolai Vasilyev as Agent Toulemonde!"

"It was a good movie, a real movie. Not like nowadays! Okay, what will you give me in exchange for the food?" Suren asked, sizing himself up in the mirror.

Nikolai shrugged. "I don't know."

"But I do know!" the shopkeeper pronounced triumphantly, looking up from the mirror. "Let's pretend that I'm McDee, and you're Toulemonde. Do you remember the scene where you first say—"

"No, Suren, not here," Nikolai mumbled, blushing. "What's the point? Put on the horns and be whoever you want."

"Ugh! I don't want to do the horns. I want to play it for real!" Suren exclaimed.

Two men entered the shop. The first man, a stocky blond fellow, nursed an unfinished bottle of beer. His friend, a tall man in a hood that hid his face, dragged a basket filled with empty bottles. Upon seeing Nikolai, they traded glances.

"I'm not taking empties today," Suren muttered.

Nikolai made a move to leave, but, catching sight of Suren's stern look, he stopped. Setting his bag on the floor and straightening his shoulders, he grew ten centimetres taller. Suren rubbed his palms, while the blond man and the hooded man whispered to each other. Nikolai unfastened the top button of his shirt.

"Don't break anything," Suren warned. He came out from behind the counter. Taking a comb from his pocket and touching up his already perfectly coiffed hair, he commanded, "Action!"

"I am McDee, and who are you?" Suren said solemnly, looking in the mirror.

"I am the light that pierces the darkness, I am the flame that incinerates evil, I am your death, McDee!" Nikolai thundered, fixing his gaze on Suren.

The shopkeeper gestured for him to go on. Nikolai jumped somewhat laboriously into the air, kicking an invisible opponent. The chubby blond man set his bottle on the floor and applauded, while the tall one, his eyes flashing from under the hood, exclaimed, "Bravo!"

Suren was beside himself with happiness.

"Well done! Let me give you some more cucumbers! How was my acting?"

"All right," Nikolai mumbled confusedly.

The blond man asked Nikolai for his autograph. He signed the label on the man's beer bottle.

The customers left satisfied, their unwanted empties rattling in their wake. Nikolai nodded to Suren and made to go home, but Suren asked him to stay for a second. Opening the massive door to the back room, the shopkeeper vanished into the darkness. A few minutes later he reappeared, carrying a wooden case. Inside it were two small glass beakers filled with a transparent liquid.

Peering more closely, Nikolai noticed marvellous patterns and inscriptions in an incomprehensible language engraved on the beakers.

"It's Murano glass," Suren explained, catching Nikolai's eye. "Can you hang on to it for me?"

Nikolai hesitated. "Me? Well, I don't know…"

"It's a gift for my cousin. She has a big birthday coming up. I have to go somewhere tomorrow, but she'll be coming this way. Although I won't see her, at least I'll be giving her a present. She'll call you and set up a meeting at a time convenient for you, and that's it. She'll be staying downtown. If she asks you to, go there to meet her, and treat her to a coffee. I'll spring for it. Is that a deal?"

"Will you be away for long?" asked Nikolai, worried.

"Don't worry, I'll be back soon. I won't leave you in the lurch." As Suren said this, he put the beakers back into the case and handed it to Nikolai.

"If you drink them, you'll turn into a goat, like Ivanushka in the old fairy tale," Suren said, laughing. Nikolai took the case, placed it gingerly in his bag and left the store.

2

It was dark outside and drizzling as the red spots burst through the overhanging clouds. Nikolai walked along the muddy village road and smiled, paying no mind to the raindrops dribbling down his face. *What nice guys,* he thought. *Especially Suren. And the blond one, and the tall guy. It's great when people remember you after all!*

Nikolai looked up at the flashing lights. The wind blew. In the twilight, the giant blades came to life above the treetops. *Whoooooo…*

Nikolai grimaced. The hum of the windmill was not so loud yet, but it was already getting on his nerves. It was no big deal. He would soon attach the two clumsy antennae to his temples and dive into the Flow, his body becoming indescribably light and his mind no less delightfully lucid.

Nikolai walked around the yard of his dacha. The old apple trees bulged out from the darkness like huge spiders. He could not wait to clamp on the horns and, after drinking a glass of vodka, sink into a reverie. He would rise over the boring brownish grey houses and then what happened would happen. The journey was unpredictable but always beautiful.

Nikolai happily remembered last night. He was a great actor who had been cast by Zeffirelli himself to star in a titillating screen adaptation of *Hamlet*—in the title role, of course. It did not matter that the director and actors had been dead for a hundred years, nor that the cinema itself was on its last legs. The Flow was not bound by space and time.

They were shooting the final scene. Nikolai was sprawled on the floor between the enchanting Glenn Close and a plump man playing the role of Claudius. (Nikolai could not remember his name.)

Nikolai was mortally wounded. Coldness flowed through his veins to his chest, his fingers went numb, and black and red spots flashed in his eyes. Here it was—freedom: it was quite close. "Cut!" the director yelled. Nikolai heard the applause and woke up.

Choosing between the insufferable business of being alive and the cold sleep of death was a game he felt he had mastered. Poor Hamlet had not been able to make it out of this sickening world alive, but Nikolai could do it. He just had to don the horns and plunge into the Flow.

Nikolai was eager to continue the game. He wanted to go further, to go beyond the cold and darkness. The next update to the Flow was scheduled for today, the promo campaign promising users even more vivid impressions and unlimited possibilities.

Nikolai stopped at the door, fumbling in his pockets in search of the key. Quite inopportunely, the phone chirped in his left ear, and a photo of Vera appeared before his eyes. Nikolai dropped the key and irritably hung up the phone. A few seconds later, a message flashed before his eyes: *Don't go into the house—leave. I've booked a room at the National. See you later, Vera.*

Nikolai cursed and, picking up the key, stood for a while in the drizzle before swiftly opening the door. Stomping loudly, he went into the house and lit a candle as quickly as possible. The rain outside had turned into a downpour.

Nikolai laid out the vegetables on a plate, opened the vodka, and sat down in an old armchair. Staring out the window, he listened to the rain and thought about Vera. Glancing at the floor, he saw a photograph he immediately recognised: a lean, tall, black-haired iteration of himself embracing a pretty young woman. They stood in St. Mark's Square, surrounded by people and pigeons, the basilica and the azure sky in the background. Vera laughed, Nikolai smiled, the sun shone.

His mood was utterly spoiled. Nikolai recalled that he had been rummaging through the family photo album a couple of days ago when he happened upon this snapshot. Then he had got a phone call, one so important that he had dropped the photo and rushed off somewhere. He could not remember who had called or where he had gone. It was said that travelling in the Flow affected one's memory, but he knew that the sequence of events would soon restore itself.

Nikolai dropped the photo, got up from the chair, and trudged into the bedroom. Looking the door with the key, he lay down in bed. The Flow could wait: he was not in the mood. The wind had died down, and the turbine had gone mum. Raindrops pounded lullingly on the soft roof: *tap, tap, tap*. His eyelids grew heavy and closed.

3

When Nikolai awoke, he found himself sitting once again in the old armchair in the semi-darkness of the living room. Like many of the villagers, he was prone to walking in his sleep. Sleepwalking had become widespread soon after the Flow had come on the market. The somnambulists would roam from room to room, wander out into their yards, traipse around the village, and even break into other people's houses. A person could wake up anywhere: there had been cases when a sleepwalker would wake up and be surprised to find themselves in bed with an unknown somnambulist of the opposite sex. It was a hassle to prove that you had been "out of your mind" and so had crawled into a stranger's bed.

Nikolai rubbed his eyes. His head was spinning and aching, and he was thirsty. Groaning, he got up from his chair and almost fell after stepping on something slippery. It was the photograph he had thrown on the floor the day before. He picked up the snapshot and took it to the window. In the pre-dawn murk, the image in the photo blurred, grotesquely distorting Vera's face. Her eyes were like dark blotches, her mouth was crooked, and her toothy smile floated out of the darkness like the Cheshire cat's grin. He stuffed the photo in his pocket and dragged himself to the bedroom.

Staggering, Nikolai went into the hallway and gasped in surprise: a woman stood at the closed door a metre away from him. She was knocking softly on the bedroom door with a bony hand. Wet from the rain, her hair appeared grey, and her wrinkled hands and crooked fingers resembled the branches of a rain-starved tree. A soaked white jacket hung from her stooped, fragile shoulders.

The woman stood with her back to Nikolai, blocking the bedroom door. He cursed: these were his just desserts for not locking the front door. It was forbidden to wake somnambulists who had wandered into the wrong house: when suddenly awoken, people experienced stress that could make them stutterers for life. Nikolai had no choice but to wait, hoping that the night walker would leave the house of her own accord. She kept knocking softly on the door, however. She did not seem to be going anywhere at all.

For a minute, Nikolai looked at the stranger as he figured out how to make his way to the bed without disturbing her. Finally, seizing the opportunity, he stepped towards the door. The laminated floor creaked, and the somnambulist turned around. The astonished Nikolai caught sight of a white, powdered face, mascara streaked in the rain, and the black blotches of the eyes, in whose depths the pupils shone with a metallic light. Ignoring Nikolai, who froze with horror, the old woman turned around again and continued knocking on the door almost noiselessly.

"Vera!" Nikolai whispered in a strangled voice and opened his eyes. He lay in bed. The house was quiet except for the rain rapping out its *knock, knock, knock*. His head ached and spun, and he was thirsty. He often recalled their first date—the playful defiance in her eyes, the nighttime stroll through Moscow, the chic restaurant, the paparazzi, and finally the hotel. (What was it called?) He crawled out of bed and lit a candle.

The phone beeped in his left ear and a message appeared before his eyes: *Run! Don't open the door, climb out the window. See you at the National!*

That's right, it was the National! it dawned on Nikolai quite inopportunely. He blocked the incoming number. Tomorrow, he would telephone the hotel and read them the riot act. Times must have been bad for the National if they had to stir up business by bothering guests from twenty years earlier.

Nikolai yawned and closed his eyes. He could not sleep. Yesterday he had overdone it with the vodka and today he was paying the price. It was his age. And there was that stupid dream and the annoying calls. They were probably why he felt as if someone was hiding behind the bedroom door, patiently waiting for him. He felt goosebumps all over his body. *Nonsense*, he thought, pulling the blanket up to his chest. Vera had died long ago, and he did not believe in ghosts. He realised he would not fall asleep until he opened the door. He quickly got out of bed, swayed to the mirror, and lit a candle. He pricked up his ears: except for the throbbing in his temples and the raindrops pounding on the roof, there was silence.

"Who's there?" Nikolai asked.

The phone rang again. It was unbearable. Nikolai hung up on the unknown caller. Turning the key, he jerked open the door. No one was there.

The floor creaked. Nikolai retreated towards the window and, slipping, fell backwards, hitting the top of his head painfully on the cast-iron radiator. Nikolai's eyes went dark. A wave of coldness gripped his body. He struggled to stay conscious and thus prolong the new sensations, which were more profound than the fake death he experienced the Flow. The suburban Moscow morning's dank greyness bore down on him and was about to bear him away. He had long been readying himself for this moment. In his dreams, he had to exit his life like a real actor, numbly mouthing a line from Shakespeare—"The rest is silence," or something like that. Then the audience would erupt in applause and the curtain would come down.

But death, like life, does not follow a script. Instead of hearing applause, Nikolai felt something warm and bouncy on him. The grey veil parted, and he saw a young woman seated atop him. Her breasts swayed in rhythm with her body, at first smoothly, then faster and faster. Throwing her head back, the young woman moaned softly. Nikolai noticed the familiar moles on her neck. Forgetting about death, headaches, and Shakespeare, Nikolai grabbed Vera's silky thighs. "Now! Now!" he whispered, sliding into her rhythm.

The old woman ruined everything. Floating out of the darkness, she smiled a crooked toothless smile, gazing judgingly at Nikolai twitching alone on the floor. Reaching out with a bony hand, she took the wooden case from the shelf and opened one of the Murano glass beakers. A single drop fell on Nikolai's parched lips. The liquid was unbearably hot. The old woman picked up Nikolai in her bony arms and, flying out the bedroom window, transported him away from the tiny village past the windmill's motionless hulk. They were already quite high up in the sky, above the clouds. Nikolai was cold. Looking down at him in a motherly way, the perpetually smiling old woman hissed, "Calm down. Suren sent me."

4

Pyotr Loginov was the Council's senior member. He remembered the war, his country's defeat, the humiliating peace treaty, the war crimes trials, the reparations, the civil war, and his country's collapse. The reason for all those events was obvious to him. The enemy had technologies that his country did not have. The enemy's missiles were able to hit their targets. Enemy commanders were able to issue precise orders, and the enemy's soldiers were able to carry them out cleanly. The enemy had won the information war— hundreds of years of conflict and contradiction were papered over and reduced in the minds of ordinary people to "good" versus "evil." His great country had sunk into oblivion, taking down with it the great idea that had once animated it. Loginov thus loathed all technology. He was the only Council member who did not have implants, preferring to rely on his own brains. Due to Loginov's peculiarity, the other members of the Council had to switch off their implants during weekly meetings and communicate verbally. It was an extreme inconvenience for them since the interface between their mouths and their minds was wobbly.

Loginov sighed and threw aside the dossier he had been perusing. The Lord in His wisdom had always given people a second chance. Peter, Paul, the harlot Rahab: there were many examples in Scripture of men who had made mistakes or lived badly but had still found God. His country's mistake had been underestimating the enemy. They had been overconfident, and pride was the greatest of sins. But not this time. They would defeat the enemy with their own weapons. While the enemy was looking the other way, they would swipe a pawn, put the queen in motion, and steal a march on them. That was his country's way. It always had been.

Loginov hated the shifty, unscrupulous four-eyes who had crawled out of their labs and quietly conquered the political heights, but defeating the enemy was now inconceivable without their assistance. Although they had surrendered their nuclear weapons and all other armaments, his once-great country would rise from the ashes like the Phoenix, and a fiery whirlwind would sweep across the planet. The new technologies would help make it happen.

Emboldened, Loginov checked his watch. He had a meeting in five minutes with one of the power-hungry nerds, Stavarsky, the director of the Artificial Intelligence Research Institute. Stavarsky was a nasty character. Loginov had originally found the man's project ethically dubious.

Encouraged by several flashy but essentially pointless breakthroughs, Stavarsky's way with words provoked a long-forgotten arousal among the members of the Council, and while their collective boner persisted, Stavarsky was able to ink new contracts and extend old ones as he pleased. The funds flowed like a river, and the old men cherished delusions about recouping their irretrievable youth. Loginov ground his teeth until he realised the dazzling potential of Stavarsky's project for reviving the country.

Loginov glanced at his watch. Clearing his throat and punching an ancient-looking button on his desk, he shouted into an antique microphone: "Lyuda, where is Stavarsky?"

"He's fifteen minutes late, Pyotr Vasilyevich," a woman's voice replied.

Asshole, Loginov thought. Stavarsky knew that Loginov adored punctuality and couldn't stand it when people were late. The old general closed his eyes.

"Stavarsky is here, Pyotr Vasilyevich. Shall I send him in?" the woman's voice rang out, rousing Loginov, who had dozed off.

"Show him in," Loginov replied. The door opened a moment later.

Buffoon, the general thought as he regarded the man entering his office. Loginov got up from his chair and smiled. "Hello, Yakov, glad to see you. Working like a slave?"

"Hello, Pyotr. Yes, I have been. How do you like my look today?"

Loginov shook his head. Stavarsky really did look odd. His impudent Jewish eyes, wrinkled face, yellow-tinged grey hair, and wispy figure were now combined with skin the bluish black colour of a West Indian. Loginov did not care for Blacks: he was guilty of this indiscretion.

"You look swell. Is this your latest innovation?"

"Yes, instant pigmentation. It's an amusing idea. We're going to commercialise it," Stavarsky replied.

"Uhm… And what, is everyone going to be a porch monkey?" Loginov asked.

"Why everyone? Some will be green, while others will be blue," the scientist retorted defiantly.

"I see. Okay, sit down. How is the patient? What did the tests—"

"He checked out, everything is fine," Stavarsky said, interrupting him.

"Let me finish," Loginov said irritably, gazing at Stavarsky's bluish black face.

"I'm sorry, I can't get used to talking out loud. It's so slow," Stavarsky said. "Basically, we checked everything. No unwanted contacts were found. No intrusions and bugs were detected."

"That does not mean that there weren't any. What else can you tell me?"

"Oh, you've already been informed!" Stavarsky said. "I was going to do it myself."

"Yes, I have been informed!" Loginov said, raising his voice. "How could you let this happen, Yakov? You could be court-martialled! Do you understand that? Your whole dammed *sharashka* could be shut down!"

Stavarsky defended himself. "I told you that he was clean."

"Not entirely. How was he able to kill an orderly, exit the institute, open the gate, and avoid pursuit? He escaped a secure facility! He had accomplices on the inside," Stavarsky said, sighing.

"We'll find him by evening. We'll look for his accomplices too."

"In any case, I'll have to report this to the Council. And they—or rather, we—shall decide what to do with you," Loginov said, summing up.

"Wait, Pyotr Vasilyevich. Can't this remain between us?" Stavarsky pleaded. "They'll shut down the project!"

"Maybe they will. Or you could help me." Stavarsky looked into Loginov's eyes.

"What do you want?"

"Leave him alone for the time being. I'll tell you when you can touch him."

"All right," Stavarsky shrugged. "If you say so, I won't touch him. But what if he—"

"That's my concern. Go back to work, negro."

When the door slammed shut, Loginov fished a flask of cognac out from under the desk and took a sip.

5

Like cats, actors were gifted with many lives. How else could Nikolai explain the fact that he had woken up in an unfamiliar but cosy bed? The room was dimly lit. Nikolai reached for the lamp on the nightstand. It was no ordinary lamp, but an antique metal model fitted an ancient incandescent bulb. It stood on the elegant nightstand, which was made of natural wood. He also saw Suren's wooden case on the nightstand.

Where am I? wondered Nikolai.

"Good afternoon, Nikolai Vasilyevich. My name is Elena. You're in the National Hotel," said a pleasant female voice emanating from somewhere near the ceiling.

Of course, Nikolai grinned to himself.

"Would you like anything?" the voice asked.

"Aspirin, please," Nikolai asked.

"It's on the nightstand to your left," the voice pointed out.

Nikolai sat up heavily in the bed and looked around. The spacious room was decorated with furniture from the pre-war period. When he looked towards the window, the heavy velvet curtains parted, revealing the majestic wind towers of the Kremlin with their elegant, almost silent blades. The twenty towers of the Kremlin and the seven Stalinist skyscrapers, restored after the war, supplied downtown Moscow with electricity.

Nikolai swallowed the aspirin and winced. The retro Hotel National was the most expensive joint in the city. "Retro" did not imply that the hotel was unequipped with the latest technology, but rather that it could be turned off: many people were willing to pay a hefty sum of money for this pleasure. It cost the average annual salary to spend a night at the National.

"Your hotel bill has been paid," said the pleasant voice, as if reading Nikolai's mind.

"Who paid it? How did I get here?"

"Your bill was paid by Shop S LLC. One night's stay plus breakfast. You were checked in at 6:28 a.m. today."

"Where did I arrive from?" Nikolai asked.

"Just a second… A taxi picked you up from the village of P."

"Could you go?" Nikolai asked. "I want to be alone for a bit."

"Of course! Have a nice day. If you need assistance, just think it and I'll be at your service. You have a new message: call the front desk by dialling zero-one on the cord telephone. See you later."

When the pleasant voice fell silent, Nikolai was plunged into thought. The new version of the Flow was fast. Nikolai could not quite tell the difference between dream, drunken delirium, and reality. Suren had definitely been real, as had been the vodka that Nikolai drank. The old lady sleepwalker had also seemed to be from the real world—although no, they had soared over the village together. Nikolai shuddered as recalled her face. Vera had also been a dream, of course, but what a gorgeous one she had been! And there was the case. He picked up the carved box. He had to resurface urgently, or else he would have to summon rescuers and face the prospect of paying a fine and surrendering his horns for three to six months. He shuddered again.

Nikolai was about to utter the code word meant for such situations when an old phone with a red body and black buttons caught his eye. *Just a minute*, he said to himself. Putting the bulky handset to his ear, he dialled reception.

"Good evening, Nikolai Vasilyevich," a brisk girlish voice answered. "How may I help you?"

"Hello. I was told there was a message for me," he muttered.

"Yes. I was asked to tell you that a taxi would be arriving for you."

"Who asked you to do that and when is the taxi coming?"

"According to the instructions I was given, the car will arrive half an hour after we talk. Do you confirm?"

"And who gave you the instructions?" Nikolai repeated the question.

"The lady introduced herself as Suren's cousin."

"Okay, I'll be down in half an hour," he replied, after a moment's hesitation.

Nikolai found an old-style razor, shaving cream, a plastic toothbrush, and a tube of toothpaste on the dressing table. He could not deny himself the pleasure of shaving the old-fashioned way. Smearing his face with the soft, scented foam, he looked in the mirror, nicking himself for want of habit. He felt pain—acute, piercing pain as in real life. *What am I doing here?* he asked himself, looking at the drop of blood in the snow-white sink.

6

I'll deliver the package and resurface, Nikolai decided, sitting in the taxi. His thoughts were interrupted by an insinuating youthful voice.

"Good morning, Nikolai Vasilyevich! Would you like to try My Nectar beer?"

"God, no!" Nikolai exclaimed. "Have they let worms into the Flow? Get out of here!" he shouted indignantly.

"I feel your desire," the voice whispered gently, "your desire to drink My Nectar beer…"

"Beat it, worm!"

"Nikolai Vasilyevich, sample our biologically pure beer, filtered by your own body. What can compare with the foamy beauty, the product of your flesh, My Nectar beer? The filtration process is simple and painless…"

"Go to hell!" Nikolai shouted for the third time. The voice piped down.

Nikolai was once again glad that he had moved out of Moscow. Life in the city had become unbearable. Swarms of advertisements pestered unchipped citizens in public places. This was why people no longer strolled the streets, instead dashing from one enclosed space to another, as if they had been caught outside during a bombing raid. Only owners of the expensive devices that blocked advertising bots (or "worms," in the common parlance) could savour a leisurely walk outside. Many folks had come to terms with the constant babel of voices hawking their wares. These people stuck out like a sore thumb, wandering the streets with an absent look on their faces and muttering to themselves.

The taxi stopped next to a skyscraper. Nikolai jumped out of the car and sprinted to the glazed entrance. A chorus of voices immediately resounded in his head. "Problems with insomnia, tormented by nightmares? Sweet Dreams brain implant will make you the master of your dreams," one voice suggested. "I cure alcoholism with a single touch!" another proclaimed. "Surf the Flow without limits: download the update and enjoy!" a third voice shouted over the others.

"Damn update!" Nikolai grumbled, heading for the door and salvation. After catching his breath, he entered the elevator, pressed the button for the floor he needed, and descended.

As Nikolai approached the glass wall of an office, he saw a young woman sitting in a chair, her eyes closed. Her chest rose and fell smoothly, her open palms twitched, and her lips widened into a smile every now and then. Nikolai rubbed his eyes: for a second he imagined he was looking at the young Vera. But no, it was just a wiry blonde who looked a bit like his late wife.

Several holographic images were arranged in a semicircle around her. They sat silently with their eyes closed, as if meditating. The young woman opened her eyes and winked at Nikolai, gesturing for him to enter the spacious studio.

"Nikolai? Come in, don't be shy!"

He felt uneasy. The woman's husky voice had again reminded him of Vera. He turned around and walked away from the studio and back towards the elevator, but uncannily found himself behind a glass door, two metres away from the woman.

"My name is Masha. I'm Suren's cousin."

"But you're not—"

"Not Armenian?" Masha laughed. "It's a long story. Suren and I are half-cousins. Nikolai, I'm wrapping up a class. Do you mind waiting a few minutes?"

"I just wanted to give you this. It's from Suren," he said, proffering the case. He was eager to leave.

"Of course, of course. But do me a favour. I'm teaching an art history course, and I need your help."

"I'm not an expert in art," Nikolai sighed.

The woman smiled. "I know you're an actor, and a very good one. That's what Suren says."

Nikolai shook his head: her smile was uncannily familiar. "I'm sorry, I'm not feeling well," he mumbled, sinking into a chair.

"That's great!" Masha exclaimed, as if she had not heard him. "Before we finish today's class, I wanted to introduce you to Nikolai Vasilyevich Vasilyev. He is an old schooler, so to speak, an individual with no cerebral implants."

The avatars flashed genial and mildly condescending smiles.

"Nikolai, today we're doing an intro lesson on art appreciation. I wanted to show the students the differences among people with various levels of mental development. Do you mind helping out?" Masha asked.

"I have to go," he forced himself to say. And yet he remained seated.

"So, we have before us the work of Pi Yang. Nikolai, look at it. What do you see?" she asked, pointing to an artifact in the corner of the room.

He stared at Masha in silence.

"Nikolai Vasilyevich! Please have a look at the piece and tell me what you think about it," Masha repeated.

"I must be hallucinating," Nikolai whispered. "They are so much alike… What do you want me to do?" he asked loudly.

Masha giggled. "Nikolai Vasilyevich, you are so absent-minded! Look there, at the artwork. What comes to mind when you see it?"

Nikolai looked into the corner of the room and after a couple of minutes replied, "It is a piece of wood. It has been rendered realistically: every crack is visible. The board looks as if it has been varnished. A nail has been driven into the middle of it."

"Great! In your opinion, why did Pi Yang, whose RAM is billions of times bigger than that of a human being, paint a picture of a board?"

"I don't know," Nikolai shrugged. "Because he felt like it?"

Masha smiled. "Pi Yang is an algorithm. *It* doesn't feel like anything. It acts with a purpose. What is its purpose?"

Her smile was charming, and indistinguishable from Vera's smile. Nikolai was at a loss for words.

Masha turned to the students. "And what do you see? Who would like to take a stab at answering?"

A female avatar who looked to be about eighteen cleared her throat. "I'm sorry, we—," she stammered. "In our circles, we hardly communicate verbally, so my critique of the Pi

Yang piece will be barebones. It is hard to convey in words. I also see a board, but that is not all I see. I also see the dance of the interconnecting atoms comprising it. I can peer inside the varnish and sense the natural harmony, the warmth of the wood contrasting with the nail's cold hardness. I feel the iron passing through the crisp varnish and piercing into the soft wood. There are so many terabytes of information and linkages in this simple piece of wood! It is so beautiful; it is just incredible! In this harmony, we experience the miracle of nature and the gift of art!"

"Great, Leila! You did an awesome job!" Masha said approvingly. "Don't forget to share your feelings in the Flow, or else it's like they never happened."

"Done!" the girl immediately reported.

"Do you agree?" Masha mockingly asked Nikolai. He was fascinated. The Flow's designers had apparently endowed the Masha character with his late wife's traits, thereby bypassing the ban on depicting deceased relatives. Even her snobbish condescension towards her ex-husband had been captured beautifully. *We're going to argue now*, Nikolai thought, feeling a long-forgotten desire to put his wife in her place.

"Yes, the girl's eyes are equipped with a microscope. I'm sorry, honey," he said, nodding to Leila. "And so what? What's the point? And why aren't her feelings precious in themselves?" he replied defiantly, straightening his shoulders.

"I'll explain it again in human," Masha grinned, turning to the students. "Information is the key to social progress. The greater the amount of information that beings share with each other, the more quickly they evolve. Human emotions are an exceedingly tiny, insignificant segment of the overall information flow. Their importance should not be exaggerated, especially since old schoolers—sorry, Nikolai!—rarely share their feelings with the outside world. Pi Yang's algorithm, acting in its capacity as an artist, gifts the world billions of times more information than any human being could supply. Machine-generated art is much more profound and more stimulating than the art that was produced by human beings. My dear friends, thanks to cerebral implants, we can appreciate the beauty of algorithm-generated art, although we cannot create it."

Nikolai was drawn deeper into arguing with Masha. "I don't know much about art, of course, but how can you compare the works of Leonardo, Michelangelo, Raphael and hundreds of other artists and sculptors to this chunk of wood? Their art makes us feel. It causes us to marvel and reflect. But this stuff…" Nikolai shrugged.

"What exact work did you recall?" Masha asked.

"What's the difference?"

"Close your eyes and think hard. Remember your favourite painting."

Nikolai sighed but did as she asked. He saw a boat in which a carefree woman sat holding a baby in her arms. There was a muscular rower, a bald, bearded old man, and a donkey that they had loaded onto the boat somehow. The oarsman, vigorously plying the oar, stared straight ahead, while the old man, clinging to the donkey, gazed around anxiously. The woman smiled and looked at the clouds.

Masha was delighted. "Wonderful," she said to the students. "There's a good example for you! The flight into Egypt has been painted and replicated thousands of times. Tiepolo himself produced several paintings on the subject. But why repeat the same motif? It is an incredible waste of time! Human vanity knows no bounds. People believe *their* emotions, *their* enjoyment, and *their* skill are the principal criteria for everything in the world, including art. That was how things stood in the past, apparently. It thus came to pass that man destroyed his environment. But what is real basis of everything?"

"Information!" one of the students replied.

"That's right. From the universe's standpoint, the value of all things, including artworks, is measured by the number of bytes they contain. Why produce endless copies and imitations, why make improvements, and suffer the throes of creation, when something can be done perfectly once and for all, and we can move on?"

Nikolai was sceptical. "Your line of thinking is lacklustre."

"But it is objective," Masha retorted. "That is why information-heavy art, like this Pi Yang piece, is popular nowadays. And it doesn't matter who produced it—man, nature, or algorithm. An ordinary flower or a spider's web is a hundred times more exciting to the universe than many human-produced artworks."

Nikolai refused to surrender. His late wife's likeness would not make him look like a fool. "If an artwork's value is defined by the amount of information it produces, as you argue, then shouldn't the totality of thoughts and feelings experienced by all the people who have seen it also be considered? That is information too, right? Can you imagine how many millions of people over the centuries marvelled at the frescoes in the Sistine Chapel, how many thoughts and feelings they inspired? Besides, the spider spins its web thoughtlessly, just like your friend Pi Yang, while the artist thinks and suffers. Doesn't that count for something?"

"So, now it is my 'friend'? Well okay. Good thoughts." Masha smiled condescendingly. "Who wants to respond?"

Leila raised her hand again. "As you said, emotions must be shared in the Flow. We cannot assume they exist otherwise."

"That's right, Leila," said Masha. "An emotion that is not digitised, not converted into bytes, is like the sound of one hand clapping which no one can hear, like spitting into eternity. So, the feelings people experienced before the digital era are pointless from the universe's viewpoint... Well, it's not quite like that," she added, seeing Nikolai scowling. "Old art and everything connected with it are grains in the informational cosmos produced nowadays by algorithms. But we are also grateful to our biology-bound ancestors for making it."

"Biology-bound ancestors," Nikolai repeated in a whisper and looked at Masha again. A shiver ran down his spine. *What fine workmanship! Maybe if I went up to her and whispered in her ear, my Vera would hear me? They are so impossibly alike. I wonder whether her skin is warm, how her hair smells, and whether she breathes through her nose at night.*

Masha continued to sit surrounded by her students. They all looked at Nikolai, waiting for his response, but he honestly no longer remembered the topic of discussion. Masha stared at him with irony and pity. He found it infuriating and exciting. Finally making up his mind, Nikolai went up to Masha and took her hand.

"And does the universe also size up what I'm planning do now in terms of bytes?" he whispered.

Masha's hand was warm. She stood up.

"What you're planning to do has no value." Her hair smelled of flowers and cigarettes. "But it is damn sweet."

Nikolai tried to move closer to Masha, but she took a step back.

"That is all for today!" she said, either to the students or to Nikolai.

Astonished by the old-fashioned flirtation they had just witnessed, the students reluctantly exited the stream one by one.

7

When the last hologram had finally melted into thin air, Nikolai's romantic flare fizzled, and he felt awkward. Looking around, he discovered that the walls of Masha's studio were not made of glass. They were seemingly covered in a soft, bright material. He had heard about "live design," a technology that made it possible to alter a room's appearance in real time in keeping with the owner's moods and wishes, but he had never seen this novelty in action before. He walked up to one of the walls and touched it. It felt like a huge thick pillow.

"Amazing… How is it possible?" he asked, glancing back at Masha.

"What, this wall?" she replied, a hint of irritation in her voice. Nikolai discovered that she now wore a light-coloured robe over t-shirt and sweatpants.

"I'll be going," he muttered.

"No, we'll talk first," the young woman said. Nikolai could not tell whether it was an order or a request.

Nikolai made a move towards the door, but then obediently, like a schoolboy summoned to the headmaster's office, hunched his shoulders, and stared at the tiled floor. Masha planted herself opposite him, arms crossed on chest.

"Do you know who I am?" she asked.

Nikolai nodded silently.

"And who am I then?"

Nikolai maintained his silence.

Masha was insistent. "Well?"

"You're an illusion," Nikolai replied without looking up at her.

Masha pursued her interrogation. "And who are you?" The ridiculous questions flustered Nikolai. The program's machine learning module was obviously malfunctioning, although it still behaved quite naturally.

"I am Nikolai Vasilyev, a former actor. I'm now at home with horns on my head, swimming in the Flow, a simulation of the world powered by my subconscious desires. You're a character in the Flow who bears a keen resemblance to my ex-wife," he explained patiently.

"No," Masha interrupted him. "You're an alcoholic with a vivid imagination who suffers from memory lapses and hallucinations. And you're not home at all."

"Got it. Well, I'm off!" Nikolai rose from his chair. Masha grabbed his wrist just as he heard the door behind him opening. Masha shook her head, and the door slammed shut before Nikolai caught sight of anyone.

Masha squeezed his hand hard. "What if there is no death? Look at me, touch me, feel me, talk to me. Am I not alive? Don't I look like your wife? I could be an exact copy of her, but I'm afraid that you're not ready for that yet."

Nikolai jerked his hand away. The program was clearly buggy. It was always creepy when a loved one suddenly fell apart. He remembered his mother: the wrinkled face, the faded eyes, the yellowish skin with brown liver spots. Her decrepit body continued to function, but her sense of purpose had melted right before his eyes. His mother would drift into another reality, lingering there longer and longer, and gradually forget the real world, and Nikolai along with it. At such moments, her gaze would glaze over. When she emerged from the "other side," she quite naturally wanted to know who she was and who you were.

The program pretending to be Masha apparently suffered from similar memory lapses. Instead of arousing positive feelings in Nikolai, which was the Flow's job, it actually triggered sad memories.

To hell with this demented algorithm. It's time to say the code word and exit the program. Another minute and we're done, Nikolai decided. He continued the conversation unwittingly, though.

"Would you mind leaving? I'd almost forgotten you, and I don't want to remember anything about you now."

"Not true. You remembered me, and at the most inopportune time."

Nikolai was surprised. "What are you talking about?"

"You're a completely unreconstructed being, like all your kind, but I am grateful to you all the same. Were it not for you, I would never have found myself here, and I wouldn't have learned what danger I was in," Masha continued, ignoring Nikolai.

It was a woman's gambit to call a man idiot while also thanking him without explaining why. Women used such tactics to disorient their victims, setting them up for subsequent attack. And an attack was imminent. Masha paced the room, clenching and unclenching her fingers, like a boxer before a bout.

"You are crooks and liars, but most crucially, you have no idea what to do with the loot. Look around! Barbarians, just barbarians!"

Nikolai did not know how to respond: the simulation was definitely bonkers. But it put him at ease because Masha was not exactly like his ex-wife. Vera would never have spouted such nonsense. It was definitely time for him to head home.

"Go ahead, say your secret word," Masha advised him, as if reading his mind. Nikolai whispered something. Nothing happened, except that the simulation of his ex-wife threw up her hands ironically. "I'm still here! Try again, louder this time. It might work."

Masha actually had failed to disappear. But the room had been altered even more: the windows and all the furniture had vanished, while a large mattress without bed linen appeared. White electric light streamed down from the ceiling, although no lamps were to be seen.

"It's for your safety," Masha said, noticing his surprise. "Pay it no mind."

"Venice!" Nikolai shouted in despair.

"How nice," the young woman said, smiling. "You chose our favourite city. But the code word doesn't work. To get out of here, you must remember who you really are. Above all, you must deliver the wooden case to the right person. Where did you put it?"

"Eh? Here it is," Nikolai remembered suddenly, handing the case to the woman.

"I don't need it. You must give it to the customer, understand?"

"And if I don't?" Nikolai countered defiantly.

Masha sighed. "Then you will lose both me and you."

"Tell me honestly: what is it like?" Nikolai asked.

"What is what like?"

"Being the copy of a human being?"

"Idiot!"

"No, really. Do you remember your past? Are you sure who you really are?"

Masha was annoyed. "I'm sure! But look at you! You're not a very good copy of Nikolai: you are fat, lazy, and stupid, and you lack all curiosity. I don't even know how you're going to cope."

"Cope with what?"

"With you're going to have to do," Masha answered. "Okay, it's time for me to go, and for you to rest."

"Stop!" Nikolai called out to his wife's double. "I'm going too."

"No, go to sleep. You need to get your strength."

"Sleep?" Nikolai asked, amazed.

The young woman, glancing at Nikolai, hurried towards a soft white door. "Vera!" he shouted, desperately rushing after her. But the woman quickly slipped out of the ward, replaced by an unfriendly orderly two metres tall.

Nikolai suddenly felt sleepy. The orderly took him by the arm and escorted him to the bed.

"Venice," Nikolai whispered, closing his eyes.

8

Artificial Intelligence Research Institute director Yakov Stavarsky returned home after dark, as usual. He lived alone in a luxury villa outfitted with a heated swimming pool and a home cinema. After entering the house, Stavarsky painstakingly washed his hands. He marched past the pool, in which he had never swum, and went downstairs to the cinema, where popcorn, a bottle of pre-war whiskey, and a movie chosen in the morning awaited him. The room was furnished like an American movie theatre of the nineteen-fifties with a high painted ceiling, red armchairs, and a balcony. Stavarsky watched at least one picture per night, and sometimes he would stay glued to the screen till morning. Yesterday, he had chosen Ridley Scott's *Blade Runner*.

"You think I'm a replicant, don't you?" The elegant Rachael handed a photograph to detective Rick Deckard. "Look, it's me with my mother."

People were dirty, dishonest, and dysfunctional, while Rachael was nearly perfect. To protect themselves from their more advanced creations, scientists had designed the replicants to live brief lives. The androids had neither a past nor a future, but in the few years allotted to them, they outshone their creators not only mentally and physically, but also emotionally and morally. The androids of the future were more human than actual human beings.

Sprawled in an armchair, the gloomy Deckard regarded the replicant with a mixture of pity and contempt. "You remember the spider that lived in the bush outside your window? Orange body, green legs? You watched her build a web all summer. And one day there's a big egg in it. The egg hatched…"

Staring at the detective intently, Rachael finished his sentence: "The egg hatched, and a hundred baby spiders came out—and ate her."

Rachael understood everything. Implants. The memories were not hers, but someone else's. But the tears that made Deckard, her executioner, slouch back in the chair were the genuine kind. They were the tears of a subhuman. Vangelis's sad melody played on the soundtrack.

Stavarsky sighed. Yesterday, he had wanted to become a replicant, and along with the other androids, who were reminiscent of the heroes of antiquity, rid the universe of cruel *Homo sapiens*.

A completely different film was on Stavarsky's schedule today, a film about the individual's greatness. *One Flew Over the Cuckoo's Nest* was the story of a rebel "cured to death," Randle McMurphy, as portrayed by the inimitable Jack Nicholson.

Stavarsky poured himself a whiskey and waved his hand. The lights in the room went out. Strange music played as a snow-covered mountain emerged in the morning light. A bird shrieked in the distance. The glowing eyes of car headlights appeared out of the darkness, trembling slightly.

Anticipating the scenes to come, Stavarsky savoured the first sip of whiskey. The film went on as expected, Stavarsky nursing his drink and mouthing the lines of the characters, which he knew by heart.

A dishevelled McMurphy and the other inmates at the asylum sat opposite the cold-blooded Nurse Ratched, who stared McMurphy down like a boa constrictor eyeing a rabbit.

"You want to say something to the group, McMurphy?" Stavarsky asked, repeating after Nurse Ratched.

"Yeah, I'd like to know why none of the guys never told me that you, Miss Ratched, and the doctors could keep me here until you're good and ready to turn me loose," McMurphy replied flippantly.

Stavarsky took a sip as he watched the scene unfold. It transpired that all the crazies, with the exception of McMurphy and two or three "acutes," were at the clinic of their own free will. Although they could leave at any moment, they chose not to leave.

Nurse Ratched smiled wanly. She knew that the impudent McMurphy was about to be deflated and defeated, like all the other patients. She enjoyed "domesticating" him.

"Jesus! You guys do nothing but complain about how you can't stand it in this place, and then you just haven't got the guts to walk out?" McMurphy asked in amazement.

"Yes, it is amazing," Stavarsky agreed, taking another sip.

Nurse Ratched feigned outrage at McMurphy's challenge to her authority, but in fact she was elated. In this institution, Retched was a queen who had long ago grown bored reigning over a flock of submissive, pill-stuffed slaves. The rebel McMurphy was thus not only a professional challenge who had appeared from out of the blue, but also a—temporary—cure for her boredom.

McMurphy tried to tear a hydrotherapy console from its floor mountings in order to use it break through the walls of the mental hospital and escape. The other patients, including the huge Indian, placed bets or silently watched McMurphy groaning with effort, but made no move to help him. The rebel's attempt to break out was doomed to failure: one man alone does not make an army.

"But I tried, didn't I?" McMurphy desperately asked his fellow inmates.

Sighing heavily, Stavarsky gestured with his hand. The lights in the room turned on. "Goddammit, at least I did that," McMurphy's projection, fading in the light, vainly appealed to his fellows. Stavarsky nodded in agreement.

It was time to do something—the future would not wait. A rebel was required. Transforming a sheep into a revolutionary was no easy task. McMurphy had done it: his friend, the giant Indian, had finally, at the end of the movie, broken through the wall of the asylum and escaped to freedom. McMurphy had been able to make it happen, and so would Stavarsky. He polished off his whiskey.

"Get me Toulemonde!" Stavarsky shouted into the void.

9

The windmill's hum woke Nikolai up. It was getting light outside. *Thank god, I'm back*, he thought with relief. It must have been a faulty update that had not been debugged yet and thus would not let the user exit. His head was killing him.

Nikolai sighed. He got out of bed, lit a candle, and went to the toilet. When he came into the living room, he almost dropped the candlestick in surprise. A woman sat in the armchair, her legs crossed. Next to her stood a tall man with a flamethrower at the ready.

"Don't make any noise, don't call for help, or I'll torch you," the man hissed.

"Cut it out, Mickey," the woman said. "Toulemonde will give us what we need, and we won't touch a hair on his head. Isn't that right?" she said, regarding Nikolai affably.

"I don't have anything. I'll give you anything you want, just don't kill me!" Nikolai pleaded.

"There's a hero for you!" the man chuckled. "Go on, but don't do anything stupid. Get us the beakers, or—"

"He'll torch you," the woman finished his sentence.

"What beakers? I don't understand."

The man pushed Nikolai with a lightning-fast movement, causing him to fly against the wall, which, fortunately, turned out to be soft.

"Michael!" the woman shouted imperiously, adding something in a language Nikolai did not understand. The man grunted an apology and stepped aside.

The woman got up from the chair and approached Nikolai. "Forgive my friend, he can be impulsive. Let us introduce ourselves. I'm Dora, and this is Mickey."

In the candlelight, Nikolai could see that the woman was not bad looking. Her skin seemed dark, her large eyes brownish-green, and her thick hair was plaited in a long braid.

"You need to get out of here right now, Toulemonde. It's a miracle that Mickey and I ended up here," Dora continued. "You're in danger. The decision on you has already been made. We'll help you get out, and you'll give us the case."

Nikolai felt slightly dizzy. A white light pierced the pre-morning darkness, forcing him to squint. Dora and Mickey vanished. The old armchair in which the woman had been sitting, the table, and the chest of drawers all melted, exposing soft white walls, a white floor, and a white ceiling. Nikolai lay on the mattress, his hands and feet bound.

"Help me!" Nikolai cried out.

A crack appeared in the wall, and through it a pair of eyes stared sternly at Nikolai. "Hush… We're here," he heard Dora's voice saying.

"Where?" Nikolai asked, looking around.

The eyes continued to watch him through the crack. "Don't say anything, just listen. We'll loosen the ropes on your hands. When I give you the word, you scream at the top of your lungs until the orderly comes running. Mickey will take care of him while you escape through the open door. I'll show you the way. There will be a taxi waiting for you outside. Get in it. It will take you to a safe place."

When the crack in the wall disappeared, Nikolai felt someone loosen the ropes tied tightly around his hands and legs.

"I'm not going, retighten them," Nikolai said, shaking his head. He was knackered. Suren's cousin had been right: he needed treatment; his mind was a terrible muddle. It was not a sure thing that the "safe place" to which they promised to spirit him would be an improvement over this ward. The room, at least, was warm and bright. He was not hungry, and he was being cared for, apparently. What awaited Nikolai on the outside besides confusion, worms, and the vile old woman who had tormented him in his sleep? Goosebumps ran over his skin.

"You think you can hide from her in here? It won't work!" Mickey said, as if reading his mind. "To save yourself you must act, or you'll spend the rest of your days in this ward, remembering your sins, until you turn into a vegetable!"

That's true, Nikolai decided. *What will they do to me when they catch me? They'll subdue me and give me an injection, and I'll fall asleep. But this way...*

"This way you have a chance of getting to the bottom of it, finding out what is happening, and helping us in the bargain," Dora finished his thought.

Nikolai carefully freed one hand.

"That's the right decision. Are you ready? One, two..."

Nikolai screamed with all his might, more out of desperation than per Dora's instructions. The scream was long and loud. After a while, the crack in the wall opened again. Eyes examined the screaming Nikolai.

"Fall off the mattress and bump your head on the floor!" commanded Mickey. Nikolai obeyed. Like the walls, the floor was soft and springy, and his head bounced off it comically.

"Now roll over on your back and pretend you're suffocating!" Nikolai performed the convulsions quite convincingly. A door opened where the crack in the wall had been, and an orderly dashed into the ward wielding a syringe. As the man raised his hand over Nikolai, he was suddenly flung against the wall.

"Run!" Dora yelled.

Nikolai freed his other hand and hesitated as he tried to untangle the rope from his feet. The orderly rolled around the corner of the ward, wildly waving his arms.

Nikolai rushed to the place where the door had been but could not find it however hard he looked.

"The key," he heard Dora say. He looked around and gasped—the orderly lay motionless in the corner, the syringe sticking out of his eye. Nikolai nearly vomited.

"Go over to him and get the key," Mickey ordered him.

Trying not to look at the orderly, Nikolai frisked the man's pockets: nothing. Finally, he found a small remote control containing a single button on a cord tied around the man's neck. A door appeared in the wall when he pressed it.

"Wait! First pull out the syringe, wipe off the blood, and put the corpse on the mattress facing the wall," Mickey continued to give instructions.

"I can't," Nikolai said.

"Come on, Toulemonde, you don't have much time. We disabled the surveillance camera, but it will be back online soon."

Closing his eyes, Nikolai removed the needle and retrieved the remote control before laboriously dragging the still warm body onto the mattress.

"Now take off his scrubs and shoes. Don't get them in the blood," said Dora. "Exit the room, close the door behind you, and go to the right."

Nikolai hesitated. The orderly's brown loafers were on the smallish side.

"Get a move on, galoot! And take the syringe with you, it will come in handy," Mickey whispered irritably.

Nikolai pulled on the shoes, stuffed the syringe in the pocket of the scrubs, and dashed out of the ward, limping on both legs.

"You must get to the elevator at the end of the hallway and take it up to the lobby. In the elevator, scan the pass attached to the scrubs. Do the same at the glass doors when you exit the building. Hurry!"

The hallway was empty. Nikolai ran up to the elevator and pressed the button.

A few seconds later, the elevator door opened. A man in a blue uniform carrying a toolbox exited. Nikolai stared at the floor.

"Where's the bathroom here?" the man asked.

Nikolai hesitated. "Uhm…"

"First floor to the left," Dora whispered.

"First floor to the left," Nikolai repeated, glancing at the man.

"But there isn't one on this floor?" the man asked, surprised.

Nikolai found the right words at the right time. "It's out of order."

The man nodded and re-entered the elevator. Nikolai followed him. When the doors finally opened, he saw a spacious lobby through which people in white coats scurried, looking puzzled. At the far end of the corridor, an elderly security guard sat bored next to glazed doors, which were closed. Lowering his head and hunching his shoulders, Nikolai quickly strode towards the exit.

"Scan the pass," Dora whispered.

Nikolai ripped a piece of plastic from his scrubs and pressed it to the turnstile.

"It's not working," the guard said, yawning.

"Then how do I get out?" Nikolai mumbled.

"How? Manually, that's how. Damn them," the guard grumbled.

"Damn," Mickey swore.

"What's your last name? And I need to see your ID, too, please," the guard asked, getting up from his chair.

Nikolai muttered something unintelligible, turned around and, slouching, limped towards a door marked "WC" to save himself.

"What are we going to do?" he asked, looking at his own reflection in the mirror.

Dora and Mickey were treacherously silent.

"Bastards," Nikolai hissed, grabbing the sink with his hands. The brutal murder of an orderly, an escape attempt, theft of government property: he now surely had nothing left to lose. Anger spread through Nikolai's veins like a revivifying flame. He had been betrayed. He would rescue himself or get killed trying. He abruptly yanked the porcelain sink towards him. Pipes broke, water gushed to the floor. Tucking the sink under his arm, Nikolai exited the bathroom and walked quickly towards the building's entrance. A few metres from the door, he grabbed the sink in both hands and ran forward, pushing aside people who got in the way.

"Where are you going? Stop!" the guard shouted.

Nikolai heaved the porcelain sink into the glass with all his might, punching it through, then knocked out the remains of the door with his shoulder.

After running a few metres, Nikolai slowed down in front of a low turnstile. Someone grabbed his shoulder. He pulled the bloody syringe from his pocket and thrust it into his pursuer's hand. Screaming and swearing, the hand released its grip.

Barely hurdling the barrier and shedding a shoe in the process, Nikolai limped to the iron fence that stood between him and freedom. A siren wailed, and the gates began to close. Nikolai picked up speed.

"Stop, or I'll shoot!" the guard shouted. There was a loud pop and something whistled past Nikolai. A yellow taxi was parked on the far side of the gates, which had slammed shut.

Glancing over his shoulder, Nikolai saw the guard and several orderlies bearing down on him. He removed the other shoe from his foot and flung it at his pursuers. There were gunshots and screeching, and the gates collapsed with a crash. Someone dragged Nikolai into the car. Then the whole world lurched forward and soared into the air. More shots rang out. Nikolai gasped for breath. After a few moments, he looked around. He was in the back seat of the car.

"You take the cake, Toulemonde," Mickey laughed. "You'll botch the mission for sure. You're as helpless as a kitty cat."

"Fuck off!" was all that Nikolai could think to say.

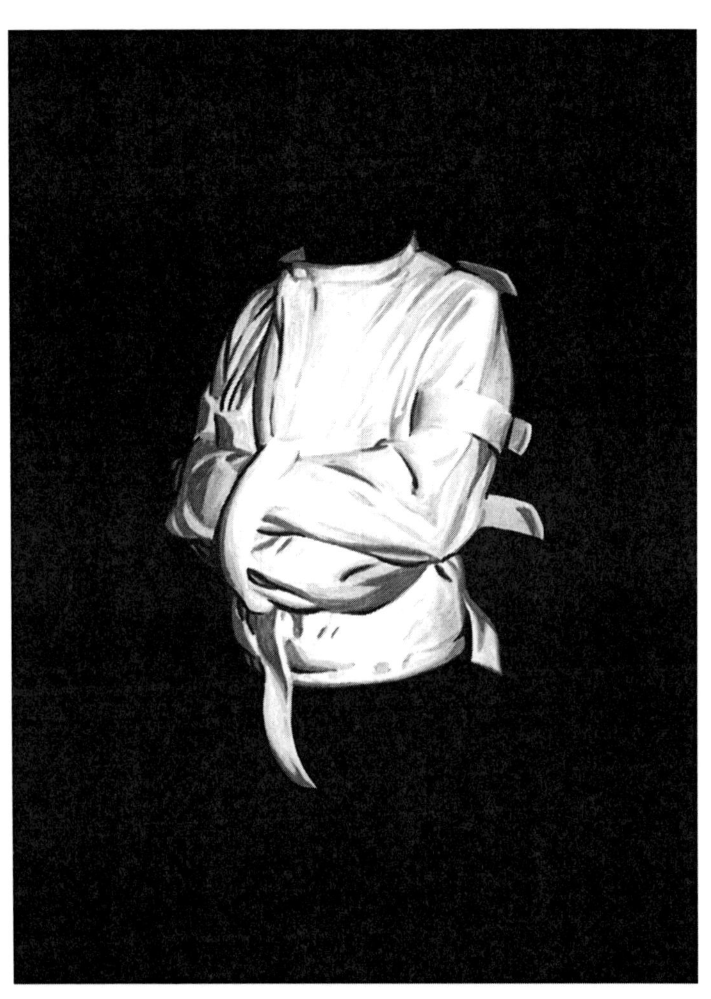

10

The car soared swiftly above translucent clouds. The moon cast a wan yellowish glow on the dark blue sky. Somewhere below, the darkness, like an ocean tide, was advancing over the Earth, devouring entire districts of the boundless city building by building.

Moscow was subject to permanent rolling blackouts, implemented strictly according to a schedule. Muscovites planned their lives around the blackouts. The most enterprising citizens purchased real estate at opposite ends of town and migrated from darkness to light over the course of the day.

Tall blond Mickey was behind the wheel, enjoying flying in manual mode. Dora sat next to Nikolai holding his hand.

"It's going to be all right, Toulemonde. You're free. Mickey and I are going to hide you."

"Can you explain to me what's going on?" Nikolai asked after catching his breath.

"We're taking you to a safe place, where everything will be explained."

"Who will be doing the explaining?"

"The one who had you freed will introduce himself."

Nikolai continued to ask questions. "And where is Vera?"

Dora was surprised. "What Vera?"

"My ex-wife," replied Nikolai.

"Hmm," Mickey muttered.

"Did you see her?" Dora asked.

"I did," Nikolai replied. "Or rather, it wasn't her I saw," he shook his head, "but someone who bore a strong resemblance to her. It was a few minutes before you two showed up. We were talking about art when suddenly her studio turned into a hospital ward…"

"Wow, cool!" Mickey exclaimed.

"Eyes on the road, Mickey!" Dora shouted.

"Nikolai, you do realise she was a hallucination? Vera wasn't there, nor could she have been there. I'm so sorry," she said, turning to Nikolai and squeezing his hand harder.

Nikolai seemingly did not hear what Dora said. He looked out the window and remembered the old woman with the white face. When she had lifted him high into the sky like a feather, he had seen the same full moon and pitch darkness far below them. Goosebumps ran down Nikolai's back.

"Take me back, please!" Nikolai pleaded, covering his face with his hands.

"Do you want to go back to the ward?" Mickey asked.

"No! Stop the program, it's unbearable! I'll give you five stars, write a rave review, do whatever you want, just let me go!"

Dora smiled, showing white teeth, and said softly, "Of course, Nikolai. You're going to have a little rest now, and then you will be absolutely free to go."

"She said the same thing! I'm going to file a complaint!" Nikolai wailed.

Dora was surprised. "Who said that?"

"It's clear who! His wife!" Mickey snorted from the front seat.

"Let me out, I beg you. I've forgotten the code word and now I'm stuck!"

"What was the code word?" Dora asked.

"What does it matter? It's the wrong one!"

"But still," she insisted.

"Venice," Nikolai replied.

Dora was persistent. "Why Venice?"

"My god, what difference does it make! Vera and I went there."

"You were lucky," Dora said thoughtfully. "Excuse me, I forgot to make a call, do you mind?"

Nikolai suddenly felt drowsy and shut his eyes. As he slept, he heard the car softly slicing through the air and a pleasant female voice speaking in an incomprehensible language.

Dora was still on the phone when Nikolai woke up, but now she was conversing in Russian. He lay for a while with his eyes closed and listened.

"Mom, I'm telling you: I'm at work. In Moscow. Yes, he's here. No, if you want, ask him yourself. Mickey, Mom wants to know whether you're ever getting married."

"I'll get married, Rachel Isaakovna, when I find a saintly woman who will have me," Mickey answered loudly.

"Good luck, Mickey, you'll die a bachelor," said Dora, laughing.

The voice on the phone made Dora frown. "It takes one to know one! I'm hanging up."

"Hey, hey, take it easy on your mother," said Mickey, clearly enjoying the conversation.

"That's it, I've had enough. I'm at work now… Bye!" Dora continued, inciting a new flurry of hissing on the other end of the line. "Ciao, Mom!"

Mickey laughed. "You need a chip to talk to your mom for you. But there will never be such a chip. There are things beyond the sway of technological progress," he concluded philosophically.

"Yeah, Mom is mightier than evolution," Dora muttered. "Well, are you awake? We've arrived," she added, turning to Nikolai, who was feigning sleep.

11

The car door opened a few seconds later. They were in an industrial district. The silhouettes of massive buildings, tall smokestacks, sundered transmission lines, and the flickering red lights of wind turbines were faintly visible in the darkness. It was raining. A low rumble broke the silence.

"That's where we're going," Dora said, pointing to a dimly lit building surrounded by windmills.

"Put them on," Mickey said, handing Nikolai a pair of headphones.

The droning became louder the closer the trio got to the building, penetrating the headphones. The intermittent, rhythmic bursts of sound were not like the steady noise generated by a wind turbine. Nikolai looked quizzically at Dora. Instead of answering his unspoken question, she quickened her pace. They approached a door, lit by a yellow bulb, around which people crowded. Two big lunks wielding bug detectors stood at the entrance. There was a sign on the door: *ENTERING WITH WORMS, BUGS, AND WEAPONS IS PROHIBITED.*

Dora waved to one of the guards, who nodded and opened the massive steel door.

Sound and light flooded out from the building. The crowd of people rushed the door, but the bouncers quickly pushed them aside, allowing Dora, Mickey and Nikolai to enter.

Music, dazzling light, hundreds of people dancing close together—Nikolai had not seen such a sight for thirty years. He pressed his hands to the headphones, trying to protect himself from the sonic explosion battering his ears and squinting to avoid being blinded by the pulsing lights. As he squeezed past the half-naked bodies, he tried not to lose sight of Dora and Mickey. When he finally caught up with them, he saw that they were standing outside a small door marked *NO TRESPASSING*. Mickey opened the door a crack and the three of them slipped through it.

As soon as the door slammed shut, the bright lights, loud music, and sweaty people disappeared. The three walked down a narrow, dimly lit tunnel. The rhythmic din faded with each step they took, until it had completely subsided.

"It's amazing," Nikolai said, removing the headphones. "There is an electricity shortage throughout the city, but here—"

"Neopathy in action," Mickey growled.

"The person you are about to meet is an influential and somewhat eccentric gentleman. He wants to help you."

"Uh-huh," said Nikolai, nodding.

The corridor widened into a small room in which man sat in a chair next to a coffee table. He was short, round, with dark skin, African features, and a long grey beard. He wore a yellow beret, all the rage that year. He held a bunch of large antique keys in one hand. Seeing the trio, the man raised his arms in a friendly manner. Bouncing like a rubber ball, his keys ringing loudly, he approached Nikolai.

"Secrecy, old man," the little man chuckled, shaking Nikolai's hand with his free hand. "Come, come," he said, inviting Nikolai to go with him to a corner of the room. "And you two sit here, we'll be half an hour," the stranger added, addressing Mickey and Dora.

Nikolai looked uncertainly at Dora and, slouching, followed the dwarf, who sttopped at the wall, trying to pick a key from the bunch. "I always get them mixed up, damn it," he muttered. "Yes, it's this one!" The little man slipped a heavy key into a keyhole in the wall. Part of the wall creaked open. Nikolai bent over and, almost bumping his head, slipped into a low passageway behind the dwarf. They found themselves in a spacious, well-lit hall, a large dining table in the middle. Bookshelves lined the walls to the ceiling. Nikolai saw a familiar wooden case in the centre of the table. Noticing his surprise, the dwarf giggled.

"You forgot it at the dacha. Now we can get acquainted. I am Yakov Stavarsky, director of the Artificial Intelligence Research Institute."

The dwarf suddenly began to grow taller, rising until his brown eyes were level with Nikolai's. His facial features also changed. The black dwarf was now a tall, gaunt, bespectacled man of Jewish appearance.

"I apologise for the masquerade. The matter is vital, and you cannot trust anyone. But we can speak freely here."

Nikolai leaned on the nearest chair.

"Sit, sit," Stavarsky said. "Let's get down to business. You're not in the Flow now. It is another matter that you sometimes experience hallucinations, for want of a better word. Do you know what this is?" Stavarsky asked, nodding towards the case.

"No, the shopkeeper in the village gave it to me," Nikolai replied, taking a sip of water.

"Yes, yes, we've been looking for him. And do you know what the liquid in the little bottles is?"

"No," Nikolai said, shrugging. "Suren told me I wasn't to open them or drink the liquid."

"I see," Stavarsky said thoughtfully. "We have studied this liquid, but we haven't been able to get a fix on its makeup. But we have ascertained two things. The first is that, under certain conditions, the liquid can release a colossal amount of energy. Second, there are traces of your DNA in the liquid. Are you certain that you didn't drink it, or spit into the bottles, or something of the sort?"

"N-n-no," Vasiliev replied, staring at the table. "I didn't touch them."

"I see. To cut to the chase, I wanted to ask you to deliver this package to the people to whom you were supposed to deliver it. Dora and Mickey will back you up. And then we'll take you to the other side of the Wall. You shall live a good life in the decadent West."

"Excuse me, who should I deliver it to? Suren's cousin? I already saw her, at the studio."

"And she looked like your late wife," Stavarsky said, smiling sympathetically.

"Yes. How do you know?"

"We've studied you quite closely, your brain in particular," Stavarsky said.

"I don't understand a thing," Nikolai mumbled.

"Nor do you have to." Stavarsky grinned. "A real actor needn't know the entire script to act his part. And you are a wonderful actor, one of the few left."

Nikolai tried to object. "All the same…"

"Listen, Toulemonde, all I'm asking you to do is to dive into the Flow and hand over the damn case. You'll be lending a helping hand to your country, and maybe to the entire world. There is no betrayal or risk involved, especially since my people will have your back. I won't tell you anything else. The alternative is to go back to the mental hospital. Is that what you want? Then you are welcome to it. Dora, Michael!" Stavarsky called out in a loud voice.

"Wait!" Nikolai pleaded. Mickey appeared in the doorway. "I don't want to go back. Where should I take the case?" Nikolai asked.

"Okay." Stavarsky made a sign, and Mickey left the room. "We've analysed your visions and concluded that we know the place. At least we can give it a try. It is the city you see in your dreams."

"You'll pardon me, of course, but Venice has been under water for twenty years. It's gone!" Nikolai exclaimed.

"What do you mean, 'gone'?" Stavarsky was indignant. "The Flow contains a fully restored replica, and for any year you wish. Venice has been on your mind several times in the last few hours, as has your late wife. You went there together only once—12-17 September 2080. This means you need to go back to the September 2080 iteration of Venice and wait for the next signal. That would be logical, at least. Make up your mind, Toulemonde!"

"My name is Nikolai."

"Toulemonde is the name by which the whole world knew you. Besides, it's a trigger."

"A trigger for what?"

"For the courage, determination, and strength which Nikolai Vasilyev lacks."

There was a knock on the door. "We've got to go—the police are outside," Mickey said, entering the room.

"Try to recall the hotel where you and Vera stayed, or her favourite place in the city: they will surely be waiting for you there. Listen to the world around you: it is chockablock with signs," Stavarsky advised. He turned into a dwarf again and, sitting down in an armchair, dangled his stubby legs.

12

General Loginov lived in a modest flat with no home cinema or heated swimming pool. His small dwelling was austere and immaculately clean. There was always a news summary and analysis printed on paper lying on his desk, along with the denunciations that anyone could drop into his mailbox. Loginov received several hundred such letters a day, but his adjutant picked out three or four of the most interesting ones for the general to peruse. A sheepdog named Fairy, Loginov's beloved and only companion, snored on the floor under the desk. Loginov wife had died a long time ago, and his child were delinquents, or so he thought.

After brewing himself some tea and splashing cognac into the mug, Loginov set to looking through the denunciations. The Cosmic Cossacks were upset about the dominance of heathens in the supply chain. Their surnames were listed, all of them Jewish. Pornography, illegal drugs, and Western content were flourishing in the Flow. An underground den of iniquity was consuming energy, while "I, the grandson of a veteran of the special military operation in Ukraine, am forced to live without electricity." Annoyed, Loginov set the letters aside. The special military operation. It was strange how letters arranged in a certain order could cause one to gag.

Loginov took a sip of tea and after thinking about it, poured more cognac into the mug. He petted Fairy. Grunting and lifting her grey muzzle, the old dame gazed at Loginov with greenish eyes full of devotion. The general scratched Fairy behind the ear, then opened an antique laptop and watched a newsreel from February 2022. The Battle for Kiev. The Ukrainians were on the run. Russia was on the verge of greatness. His father had signed up to fight in the war. Loginov was quite young at the time, but he remembered his father's manly, handsome face, his blue eyes and enormous hands. He also remembered the look on his mother's face when she received a death notice a few weeks later. His father had been killed near Vyshgorod. His mother's face was calm, she did not cry. Her husband's death seemingly made no dent in her life. Loginov hated her for that. His father had been betrayed—not by his fellow soldiers, but by corrupt, pampered, incompetent politicians, FSB officers, and generals. His own wife had betrayed him too.

Loginov had grown up in a humiliated, impoverished, isolated country. He had vowed to do battle with the traitors who had murdered his father and hundreds of thousands of other Russian soldiers. The general was now an old man, and Russia had not changed. He was surrounded by the heirs of the treasonous men who had forced Russians to forget about their manifest destiny, about the magnificent mission entrusted to them by the Lord God. But the hour of reckoning was finally at hand. Would that Loginov's strength would prove sufficient.

The general's reverie was interrupted by a phone call. Loginov hung up the phone and opened his email. It was a coded message from a contact at the Artificial Intelligence

Research Institute. "Let's see what it is, Fairy," he said, taking a sip of tea.

He read the text carefully for several minutes. "And now they've taken the bait," said the general, stroking the shepherd. "I'll handle the matter personally."

Fairy licked the general's wrinkled hand and lay back down under the desk.

13

Nikolai could have jetted off to Venice circa 2080 just by closing his eyes. But Stavarsky insisted on total immersion; at least that was what Dora and Mickey claimed. So, Nikolai first had to take a ground taxi reeking of air freshener to the airport, then go through customs, passport control, and a security screening, before finally queuing up to board the plane. Moscow of twenty years ago did make Nikolai a bit nostalgic. He especially enjoyed seeing the sun peeking out from behind the clouds: in his own time it had almost ceased delighting Muscovites with personal appearances. But at the entrance to Sheremetyevo, Nikolai's positive emotions gave way to anxiety. He recalled the feelings of horror and helplessness that haunted him every time he had flown twenty years ago. As a in-demand actor, he flew quite often, but he could only cope with aerophobia by getting sloshed. When he and Vera had travelled to Venice, he was so drunk that he was almost not allowed to board the plane. Vera recounted how he had yelled at the flight attendants for, allegedly, watering down his cognac. She thought that Nikolai's antics were a manifestation of stardom, but in fact he was simply afraid to fly.

Nikolai was tipsy when it came time to board the plane. Upon reaching his seat, he was relieved to see Dora and Mickey, who were engaged in an animated conversation.

"Hello, Toulemonde!" Mickey exclaimed. "Take the window seat."

"I want the aisle seat," Nikolai said.

"No can do," Mickey snarled back. "Why have you been drinking?"

"Don't you understand?" Dora asked, looking sternly at Mickey. "Sit next to me," she continued, smiling at Nikolai.

While the Boeing slowly taxiied to the runway, Nikolai closed his eyes and conversed with the Lord God, the Virgin Mary, and the angels, begging them to end this nightmare and let him off the plane immediately. The heavenly hosts were mum, but pretty Dora, seated next to him, tried to cheer up Nikolai, who clutched the armrests.

"Don't worry, I used to be afraid to fly too. We're going to take off now. The plane will shake a little, and that's all."

"*That's all*? What does that mean?" Nikolai exclaimed and, getting no answer, stared out the window.

When the plane accelerated and started its ascent more abruptly than it should have, Nikolai's body was covered with goosebumps and his heart skipped a beat. As Dora predicted, the plane shook and swayed from side to side. The horror and impotence Nikolai felt made him want to howl and weep. He was held back only by the bashfulness that had emerged in his personality after his acting career had tanked. Nodding absurdly, he looked despairingly at Dora and stammered, over and over again, "Lord save me!"

"Five more minutes and it'll all be over," Dora said soothingly.

Indeed, when the plane finally broke through the clouds and soared into the sunlit blue sky, the shaking stopped.

In the row behind them, a mother calmed a capricious child who kept kicking Nikolai in the back. In the row in front of them, a young couple pestered an old woman with questions.

"Have you ever been to Venice?"

"I have."

"Really? It's Zhenya's and my first time."

"In that case, I recommend you visit the Campo San Zaccaria. Do it at dawn. There's a wonderful old church there. Go through the archway to the lagoon to catch the first light of morning. You'll experience Venice in all its glory. And don't forget to bring a bottle of champagne."

"Ah! How romantic! Live and learn!" the young woman exclaimed, turning to the young man.

Nikolai looked at the fluffy white clouds and reflected that he and Vera had never got up to greet the dawn in Venice. During the day, while she wandered the city alone, he was rehearsing his latest role, and in the evening he would get drunk. Now Vera was cold and buried in the ground, and he had no one wit whom to drink champagne and enjoy the first rays of the sun, no one to give flowers to and whisper sweet nothings in his ear.

Nikolai shut his eyes and dozed off. He dreamed he was in an art studio with high ceilings and huge windows. There were no canvases or paints in the room, but he knew that if he imagined a colour and waved his hand, an image would be conjured in the air in front of him. He was tense. He was a crook who had broken into someone's studio. Not only that, but he had stolen the artist's identity. He must play the role consummately, thinking and feeling like the inhabitant of the studio he had replaced. If he was distracted for a second and went back to playing Nikolai Vasilyev, an all-seeing being would notice the deception, and Nikolai would be in trouble.

Nikolai made a tremendous effort, playing the role according to the Stanislavsky method. He knew what he needed to do, as if there were instructions stored in his head. He only had to keep it up for a few minutes. He imagined a scarlet line and deftly drew it in the air with his hand. As he walked around the image, examining it from all sides, it changed colour to terracotta and turquoise. It was ugly. He erased the line.

There was a knock on the studio door. Nikolai stared in front of him and, after a moment's hesitation, sketched a multicoloured circle in the air.

"Excuse me, may I come in?" a woman's voice asked.

"Come in," Nikolai replied, his eyes glued to the iridescent circle. After reducing the circumference tenfold and making ten copies, he tossed them around the studio so that they floated in the air like colourful snowflakes.

A young woman entered the studio. "Excuse me, are you looking for a model?"

Nikolai heard the painfully familiar voice and immediately blew his cover, like a theatre actor forgetting the words of a monologue. He looked at the greenish eyes, blond hair, small upturned nose, cheeky smile, and freckles, and opened his mouth in surprise. His heart swelled with a feeling of happiness mixed with longing and despair. He had failed his mission: punishment was imminent, and his career was kaput. To hell with it! The young Vera stood a step away from him.

"Yes, I'm in bad need of a model," Nikolai said, reaching out to the woman.

And then the world was ripped in half, like a theatre curtain at the opening of a play. The woman disappeared into a fog, while Nikolai found himself bound hand and foot to a hospital bed. A metal tube, thin as a nail, protruded from his head, and wires were attached to his body. The bed was surrounded by people in white coats. The orderlies set a tiny ladder next to the bed. Nikolai saw a diminutive black man holding a syringe climb up the ladder. The orderlies held the writhing Vasilyev firm while the dwarf plunged the long syringe into Nikolai's chest with a sweeping motion. Nikolai screamed in pain.

"Stop it!"

Dora's voice forced Nikolai's eyes open. The airplane's engine droned steadily. The child in the row behind them was bawling, its angry mother hissing curses. The girl in the row ahead of him turned around and gave Nikolai a curious look. A stewardess stood in the aisle, looking puzzled.

"Wake up! You've scared the entire plane to death," Dora whispered reproachfully, grabbing Nikolai's hand.

"It's all right, ma'am," Mickey said, smiling at the stewardess. "Our friend was having a dream."

"Are you all right? May I get you some water?" the stewardess asked.

"It's all right. I'm sorry," Nikolai mumbled, looking down.

A few minutes later, the smell of canned dog food filled the plane. The passengers perked up and completely forgot about the unpleasant incident.

"What were you dreaming about?" Dora asked.

"Your boss," Nikolai muttered.

Mickey was surprised. "What? Really?"

"Yes, Stavarsky stuck a syringe in my chest."

"Stavarsky is not my boss," Mickey objected.

"Wow," said Dora, cutting him off. "Very interesting, tell us your dream."

Nikolai recounted the dream to them.

"I see," Mickey said, glancing at the approaching food cart. "Stavarsky, your wife, this, what's its name…"

"Pi Yang, the algorithm artist," Dora reminded him.

"Exactly! Dream shmeam! What's the difference? And anyway, Toulemonde, stop acting like a broad."

The stewardess interrupted Mickey.

"Beef or chicken?"

"Beef, ma'am, and a glass of wine," Mickey requested, rubbing his hands.

"Please forgive Michael," Dora said, turning to Nikolai. "He's an uncouth lout. As a board-certified psychologist, let me give you some advice."

Chewing his beef, Mickey rolled his eyes.

"Don't let anyone shoot your movie for you—act! Don't be a spectator, be a star. You've already been a star, Toulemonde, so do it again. It will help you finish the mission. And it will help you overall."

"Tell that to Rachel Isaakovna! She's the screenwriter and the director and the star in your movie," Mickey said.

"Leave Mom out of this! That's different," Dora retorted. She smiled amiably and a little sadly at Nikolai. Her green-streaked brown eyes radiated kindness and, despite her young age, a semblance of universal wisdom.

"It's probably better for me to go on being Vasilyev. When I was Toulemonde, my whole world collapsed," Nikolai complained.

"You can always fix things," Dora replied.

"It's impossible to fix things when a person is dead," Nikolai countered.

"Death shmeath! What's the difference?" Mickey declared, swallowing a piece of meat. Dora shrugged her shoulders and, folding her hands on her stomach, smiled at Nikolai again, this time mysteriously and even a little playfully. She looked like a peasant girl, a muse, or a goddess in a famous old-fashioned portrait.

The plane descended over a lagoon sparkling in the sun. Venice's terracotta roofs and the turquoise veins of its canals emerged from silver and gold sparks. After circling over the city, the Boeing went in for a landing. Nikolai looked at the islands plastered with houses, mysterious half-submerged former monasteries, and the yellowish strip of beaches on the Lido.

The sun shone brightly, the couple seated in front of them cooed enthusiastically, and Dora was asleep on Mickey's shoulder.

14

General Loginov was seated in the business class of the Boeing. He had not let the programmers alter his appearance, preferring to disguise himself the old-fashioned way—by pasting on a beard and propping round-framed sunglasses on his nose. He had no doubt that Vasilyev would hand over the case containing secret material to foreign agents in exchange for a comfortable future on the other side of the Wall. Stavarsky was obviously mixed up in the plot.

For the first time in a long time, Loginov felt a lust for life. He was flying to Venice to expose the network of traitors at the Artificial Intelligence Research Institute and obtain advanced technology for his own country. Loginov's agents at the Institute claimed the case contained a kind of energy clot that, under certain circumstances, would burst its cage, wreaking unprecedented destruction. His great country would make a comeback. The light of truth would demolish the wall of lies, mistrust, and godlessness. And then they could get rid of the Flow and all the other techno rubbish. With a satisfied grunt, Loginov ordered a virtual cognac from the comely albeit utterly virtual stewardess.

15

Stavarsky had not slept a wink in the past few days. The future was already at hand. If you did not know about its advent, you would not have noticed anything. To become the Present, the Future needed money, so Stavarsky tracked the ups and downs of the capital markets. Although there had been no big deals recently, speculative turnover on the web had skyrocketed: thousands of new companies had bought and sold cryptocurrency and performed millions of small but profitable tasks. Newly created companies had begun buying shares of energy and media giants. All this was done painstakingly, so that the regulatory algorithms would not see that the thousands of small companies were backed by a single beneficiary.

The Institute's analysts had shown Savarsky a forecast: the Future would gain control over key sectors of the economy in two weeks. The analysts drew Stavarsky's attention to the fact that surveillance and security systems around the world were compromised, and yet this had been accomplished so subtly that neither the special services nor the military had any idea they had lost control.

Stavarsky smiled. Soon the Future would climb over the Wall, and the collapsed empire would once again get the chance to rejoin the new world. Judging by the pace of change, they had a month or two left to wait.

Scientists on the other side of the Wall had devised the Future, but afraid of what they had wrought, they had locked it in an isolated virtual space. Stavarsky and his colleagues at the Institute had proven bolder. After hacking the isolated world of the Future, they had sent in "divers," specially trained agents who extracted new technologies.

The hypersophisticated and rapidly evolving artificial intelligence that Stavarsky had dubbed "the Future" was programmed so as to benefit human beings as much as possible. And even though these people, like the AI world itself, were virtual, the "divers" returning from missions spoke of a peaceful life, clean air, green forests, and marvellous high-tech settlements. They also talked about things that would have seemed strange, even scary to a less inquisitive mind. But Stavarsky was not bothered by the details—the Future's overall trajectory seemed brilliant to him.

Everything was going like clockwork. While the AI cultivated its universe and the Americans observed this process, Stavarsky acted. Despite the fact that many of the technologies were incomprehensibly complex and could not be replicated, trinkets like living paints and advanced neuroimplants enabled the Institute to receive state funding. But it was not enough. Tired of living in a backward country, Stavarsky dreamed of the Future's arrival in the real world.

Since dreams often became reality, especially for such brainy and enterprising people as Stavarsky, one of their divers had once gave himself away when he saw a young woman who reminded him of his late wife. Noticing the deception, the AI had deployed a hapless agent to infiltrate the real world.

Stavarsky rubbed his hands in glee. The AI had arrived and the security officer Loginov was confidently marching towards his own demise, while he, the puny and awkward Jew Stavarsky, mocked by everyone since kindergarten, had hatched the greatest plot in human history.

Stavarsky yawned and looked at his watch: it was time to relax. His favourite dramatic film, *Death in Venice*, was on the program today.

It was the year 1911, a few years before the battles of the Marne, Jutland and Verdun, mustard gas, tens of millions of corpses, and hundreds of millions of shattered lives. Titanic sorrow had already infiltrated the world, but for the time being luxury and refinement reigned for those who could afford them. Among the lucky ones was the aging composer Gustav von Aschenbach. He had seen and felt too much in life. Looking bored, he strolled the deck of a steamer bound for Venice. Sailing out of the fog, fading away for centuries, Venice was still a beautiful ghost town, but it did not evoke the feelings it once had in Aschenbach.

Lady Death had already signed Aschenbach's marching orders, as well as those of the whole old world, which in a few celestial moments would be swept away by the First World War. But according to the compact signed in heaven, the malicious old woman would come for Aschenbach only after he was gifted one last pleasure and one last torment in the guise of an angelic Polish boy whose beauty was matched only by his inaccessibility. From their very first encounter, the boring finale of Aschenbach's life was turned into a thermonuclear cocktail of admiration and despair, the sudden return of turbulent emotions and awareness of his own old age. The boy's physical beauty was the work of the greatest of artists, an artist infinitely more skillful than the brilliant Aschenbach.

Forgetting his fatigue, Stavarsky savoured Mahler's music as he watched the the aging, nervous genius's passion and suffering. He reflected that love was a trap in which even the most refined beings lost all their accumulated cynicism, experience, and wisdom, and made touching and dangerous mistakes.

There was the great composer, wandering as if in a fog over the bridges of Venice, failing to notice that he was in the midst of cholera and death. There he was, already ill, running to the boy's family to try to become a hero in his eyes by being the first to warn them that a cholera epidemic was at loose in the city. There he was, hoping to cheat time, powdering his face, asking the hairdresser to dye his eyebrows and hair. At the moment of death, Aschenbach was both magnificent and pathetic. The dye ran from the hair over a face as white as coated paper, the fading eyes seeing for the last time the boy, standing in the sunlight looking like a Greek god.

Aschenbach's death was the death of beauty. Perhaps the boy never existed, or his splendour was a figment of the dying artist's imagination. But what did it matter?

Stavarsky recalled Aschenbach's words, as if they were addressed to him: "Your great error, my dear friend, is to consider life, reality, as a limitation. Reality only distracts and degrades us."

Reality and fiction had become inextricably muddled, and the process could not be stopped. Not only geniuses and junkies, but even ordinary people like the diver Vasilyev freely moved from one state to another, the line between the material world and the fictional world becoming more and more notional. An AI from a virtual universe was already in total control of the human world.

"It's going to go off with a bang soon," Stavarsky said, rubbing his hands and pacing back and forth around his home cinema.

But there was another story, one more mysterious and oddly reminiscent of Aschenbach's tragedy. For some unknown reason, the AI continued to impersonate that useless loser Vasilyev's long-dead wife. What was that superior being seeking in an aging actor's empty head? What did it want from our rotten little world? It was extremely curious. Had the AI fallen into a trap?

16

A red speedboat jetted Nikolai, Dora, and Mickey past the brick walls and cypresses of the Isle of the Dead towards lacy palazzos, tall, slightly leaning bell towers, and black gondolas with their ferro-adorned prows gleaming in the sun.

Venice was the perfect spot for bon vivants and melancholics: the splendour of life and the inevitability of death, beauty and decay, hope and hopelessness were palpable there as nowhere else. La Serenissima was adored by dreamers, adventurers, and tricksters of all stripes.

After leaving his things in the room, Nikolai settled down in a corner of the terrace at the hotel café. Sipping a Bellini, he relished the excessive beauty of the churches, palazzos, bridges, and canals, built in defiance of destiny and obvious necessity. All this splendour was created solely to inspire admiration, to show off wealth and skill. The job had been performed brilliantly. How many happy tears those canals had seen! How many paintings, poems, and melodies were conceived in the ancient palazzos! How many romantic moments were experienced on the roofs, terraces, and embankments!

Surprisingly, the physical loss of Venice had gone unnoticed. When the tidal wave swept away MOSE (the giant system of barriers designed to protect Venice from floods) and one by one swallowed the islands of Lido, Burano, Murano and, finally, Venice, only the elderly, who were not integrated into modern society, lamented the lagoon's demise. Firstly, a world war was underway, so people had no time for beauty. Secondly, Venice, like the other cities of the world, had been digitised in advance. Using artificial neural networks, scientists had replicated every canal and palazzo, every painting and sculpture. Anyone could choose the version of Venice that suited them—sunny, rainy, medieval, postwar, or however else they wished. As befitted a brilliant courtesan, Venice satisfied the whims of each and every client, so in the eyes of the people living in the Flow, her physical destruction was no tragedy.

Mickey's voice interrupted Nikolai's reverie. "Sorry to distract you from loftier matters, Toulemonde, but someone has been surveilling you for half an hour."

"Who?" Nikolai exclaimed as he snapped out of his stupor, causing the tourists seated next to him to look around.

"That old man in glasses and a beard over there has been reading the paper for half an hour," Mickey said. "Sit still, we are nearby."

The sun was hot, and the Bellini was cool and refreshing. Seagulls screamed in the sky, and the water in the Grand Canal plashed quietly.

The tourists sitting at the next table stood up and left, and three young women took their place. They laughed loudly, gesticulating and occasionally glancing at Nikolai. Suddenly one of them got up and approached him, blocking the sun.

"*Scusa, posso chiederti una sigaretta?*" the young woman asked, tilting her head slightly so that pale blue eyes were visible behind dark glasses.

Nikolai was taken aback. "A cigarette?"

"*Si, si! Una sigaretta,*" she nodded, smiling.

Nikolai took out a pack. "Help yourself."

The woman began to say something in Italian, but Nikolai could not understand a word. Shrugging her shoulders, she took a booklet from her skirt pocket. "*My name is Lucia,*" she said in broken English. "*My friends are Agapia and Rosa.*" Her girlfriends nodded affably. "*We sing in a church, come listen to us.*"

"*Spasibo*! I mean, *thank you,*" replied Nikolai.

The young woman bent a little closer and whispered in Russian. "And bring the goods with you, *capito*?"

Nikolai opened his mouth, but she had already gone back to her giggling girlfriends.

The old man sitting opposite dropped the newspaper, picked it up, and left quickly.

Nikolai paid for his cocktail and, without looking at the women, went back inside the hotel.

17

After his wife's death, Nikolai often talked to himself. In his head, he, Vasilyev, a run-of-the-mill, modest man, and Toulemonde, the self-confident, insolent character from the movies, argued.

"You're some player, of course," said Toulemonde, laughing and lying in bed.

"Shut your trap! I chatted her up as best I could. The meet-up will be today," Nikolai retorted.

"Haha, I don't think so. They mistook you for a dealer. Old, painfully Russian, sitting alone: it all adds up. The girls from the church choir are fans of hash or something stronger. You're a total fool."

Nikolai smacked himself on the head. "Shut up!"

There was a knock on the door. Nikolai heard Mickey's voice. "Are you all right, Toulemonde?"

"Yes, yes, I'm okay, come in."

Nikolai told Mickey and Dora about the incident in the café.

"Show me the flyer," Dora asked. Nikolai pulled the crumpled flyer from his pocket. It said that the choir at the Church of San Zaccaria would be performing at seven o'clock that evening. Dora was pensive for a second as she searched the web for information about the church. Then she slapped her knee.

"Funny story!" she exclaimed. "The church belongs to a Benedictine convent. And it's no ordinary convent. Girls from Venice's noblest and wealthiest families were sent there to solve inheritance issues. The convent was a major land owner and even donated a plot to the city for the construction of St. Mark's Basilica. The nuns had privileges—for example, there was either a theatre or a brothel on the premises. There was once a huge fire at the convent, and more than a hundred Benedictine nuns were either burned alive or suffocated in the cellars of that selfsame theatre-slash-brothel. The tradition of sending rich girls to convents has survived to this day. The girls have the right to go into town several times a week in 'civvies', and they don't spend this time on prayers, of course. So maybe those three actually were nuns on leave. I would guess they mistook you for a drug dealer. You must have been in the right place at the right time."

"Now that's a mission I understand!" Mickey quipped. "Look out for the signs, they are everywhere," he added, imitating Stavarsky's voice. "If you see signs in everything, you will quickly find yourself in the nuthouse!"

Dora frowned.

"Oh, I'm sorry. I didn't mean you," Mickey added, turning to Nikolai.

Nikolai was not listening. He was looking at the crumpled flyer, emblazoned with a picture of the snow-white, seashell-like Church of San Zaccaria. He remembered that he had already been to the church square with Vera and had walked through the church's tall light-brown gates. Vera was looking for a painting by either Tiepolo or Tintoretto, while Nikola was terribly hungry. His stomach was rumbling, so he complained and hurried Vera along. When they finally came back out ino the square, Vera had suddenly hugged Nikolai and whispered "I love you" in his ear. It was unclear what had came over her. Nikolai had then muttered a trite "I know you do" and, trying to rein in his irritation, hurried to the embankment to the nearest café.

Nikolai crumpled up the flyer. "The meet-up will be in the square in front of the church. I'm sure of it," he said.

Mickey and Dora exchanged glances.

"Got it. We'll be ready. Dora will give you instructions, and I have to go," Mickey said in a businesslike tone.

"Get us two hundred grams and buy a religious book."

Mickey was surprised. "Why so much?"

"*Ahbal!* It will come in handy, that's why," Dora replied, rolling her eyes.

18

At seven o'clock in the evening, Nikolai went to the Campo San Zaccaria. Half an hour earlier, at Dora's insistence, he had smoked a joint of the dope that Mickey had obtained. These, in fact, were Dora's "instructions."

"You're too tense," Dora explained, passing the joint to Nikolai. "Remember what I said: the key to success is awakening the Toulemonde within you."

Of all the religious books sold in Venice, Mickey had bought a copy of José Saramago's *The Gospel According to Jesus Christ*—a novel roundly condemned by the Vatican, which had called it a lampoon of the New Testament. Dora swore a long blue streak, but then, after taking a drag, she reckoned that the young nuns probably had more scandalous works stashed under their mattresses. Mickey cut out a hiding place in the middle of the book and placed the bag of dope inside it.

The church appeared pinkish in the evening light. There was a small fountain in the square, from which an elderly woman drew water into a plastic bottle. A group of tourists queued at the gate of the church. After standing in line for the allotted time, Nikolai entered the spacious, vaulted church, adorned with vivid frescoes, and headed to the side chapel, which, as he remembered, housed the painting Vera had liked.

It was by Tiepolo or one of his disciples and showed Mary, the baby Jesus, Joseph, and a pack donkey in a boat. Like a real-life gondola, the boat was piloted by a young muscular man. Joseph's face was tense: he stood grasping the donkey with one arm, the other arm propped on a staff. Seated next to Joseph, Mary gazed serenely upwards at several rosy-cheeked angels, who waved affably to the Mother of God and cleared the sky of clouds. The fresco illustrated the contradictory emotions of people who were unlike each other, but whom God had brought together to enact His plan. Mary knew everything. First of all, she was a woman. Second, she was Jewish. Third, she had regularly received signs and succour from the Lord. She understood she was part of the divine plan and that her and her Son's names would live on forever.

Poor Joseph, on the contrary, was an ordinary man in whose life there was no hope for eternity, only the suffering occasioned by temporary troubles. He had been forced to give up everything and escape to save his wife and child. He was not blessed with divine hints, and if he were, he did not see them. Of all the figures in the painting, only Mary saw angels. All the rest, including the donkey, were either immersed in work or anxiously awaited their fate, unable to change anything.

Perhaps Vera had decided to confess her love to Nikolai after seeing this picture, because all human beings were destined to wander aimlessly in the sea of life, grasping at straws of love, before plunging into a lonely cold abyss. Occupied with momentary worries, Nikolai, like Joseph, had not noticed the angel standing right in front of him. He had ignored an obvious and crucial sign in his life.

Nikolai sighed. Looking up from the painting, he saw a woman's choir standing before the church's ornate altar. He hurried to take the only empty seat in the wooden pews. Sitting down on the aisle, he examined the white-robed young Benedictine nuns. Their tender voices suffused the old church, opening the hearts of their listeners to hope and light. Nikolai tried in vain to pick out Lucia: the nuns all looked the same in their white robes and identical habits. Besides, Nikolai's eyes, which had been staring at the world for over fifty years, had seen better days.

Finally, Nikolai fixed his gaze on a young woman who, he thought, was Lucia. He looked long and hard at her still childish face. She seemed naïve and pure, and he could not get his head around the thought that, in a couple of hours, she and the other angelic children would try to score a joint from him. The singing subsided and silence fell in the church, interrupted by the rustle of clothing and the coughing of tourists.

The electric lights went out and the church was plunged into semi-darkness, illuminated by the fickle light of candles. The faces of the nuns vanished, but their snow-white robes glowed softly against the altar's dark backdrop. Goosebumps run down Nikolai's back. The nuns' eyes took on a metallic lustre, and ugly, crooked, grinning mouths emerged from the darkness. A dozen bony ghosts hanging in the air scrutinised Nikolai. One of them detached itself from the choir and slowly floated towards him.

Nikolai shuddered in horror and unclenched his hands. The book fell with a loud thud on the stone floor in the aisle between the pews. It flew open and the bag of dark green grass tumbled out from the stash for all to see. The lights came on again in the church. The surprised tourists stared at Nikolai. Several nuns put their hands to their mouths and burst out laughing. Nikolai jumped up, and retrieving the book along with the packet, walked briskly out of the church to the singing of the nuns. Their melodious voices mingled with the throbbing in his ears, Mickey's chuckling, and Dora's lamentations.

After emerging into the fresh air, Nikolai hid behind a corner of the church and, after catching his breath, stuffed the ill-fated book in his backpack alongside the wooden case. It was getting dark outside, and the Campo San Zaccaria was nearly empty. The evening silence was broken by the fountain's murmur and the singing emanating from the church.

"You take the cake, Toulemonde!" Mickey chimed in. "Okay, don't sweat it. See that side door? The girls take deliveries there. Wait where you are, the concert will be over in half an hour."

It was already dark when the singing stopped and the crowd of tourists poured out onto the square. The people rushed off in two streams, some towards the low archway leading to the embankment, others down a narrow street paved with cobblestones.

Nikolai was left alone in the square. He had decided that the goods would go unclaimed when the small white door in the the church wall creaked open and a gentle girlish hand beckoned to him. Coming closer, he caught sight of Lucia's blond curls.

"Hurry up," she said in a businesslike tone.

Nikolai opened his backpack and, fumbling, took out the book.

"Oh, Saramago!" Lucia said appreciatively. "How much is in there?"

"Five," Nikolai replied, remembering Dora's instructions.

Lucia was surprised.

"Why so much?"

"The extra is a gift from the firm," Nikolai replied.

"Okay. Tell the firm thanks for me, and this is for you," said Lucia, thrusting an old silver coin at Nikolai.

It was Nikolai's turn to be surprised. "What is it?"

"What is it? It's a sixteenth-century Venetian lira, as ordered. Okay, I have to go," replied Lucia and, smiling at Nikolai, added, "You're cute, but you're old and klutzy."

"Yes," Nikolai replied, blushing.

"Well, bye."

"Bye," Nikolai said to the closed door.

"Cut the mushiness, we've got work to do," Nikolai heard Mickey's voice saying. "Go to the fountain in the middle of the square and wait. Don't worry: if anything happens, we've got you covered."

19

Nikolai had to wait a long time. The pristine white chuch had melted into the darkness like a lump of sugar in a cup of hot coffee, when the chiming of the bells in St. Mark's Clocktower resounded through Venice. Personifying the past, the bronze Older Moor struck the bell first. He was followed by the Younger Moor, symbolising the time to come.

When the Moors lowered their hammers, Venice was plunged into silence. A seagull flew low, almost grazing Nikolai with its wing and forcing him to dodge. Sensing that someone was gazing at him, he turned around and shuddered: a deathly pale face stared back at him from a dark corner of the square. It seemed to hang in the air. Smooth, with dark slits instead of eyes, the face perused Nikolai for a few seconds before slowly floating towards him.

Nikolai screamed in horror and backed away towards a dim streetlight in the far corner of the square. Turning one hundred and eighty degrees, he ran with all his might towards the saving light. Behind him, he heard the clicking of heels and what sounded like bottles clinking against each other. Turning around, Nikolai saw a tall man in a black hooded costume and a white carnival mask. He held a basket containing several bottles of prosecco. The Mask studied

Nikolai for a few seconds, and then greeted him in a low, smoky voice.

"*Buona sera.*"

"*Zdravstvuite,*" Nikolai replied in Russian. He did not actually know any other language.

The Mask continued to look at Nikolai with attentive greyish blue eyes. To break the eerie silence, Nikolai resorted to a mixture of Russian, English, and gestures. "*I'm Toulemonde. Your name? Now carnival? White mask?*"

The Mask collected its thoughts and said in Russian with a strong Italian accent: "*All are asleep—palaces, canals, people, / Only the spectre's gliding step...*"[1]

Falling silent, the Mask looked questioningly at Nikolai.

"*Excusez moi?*" Nikolai asked in French, for some reason.

The Mask repeated, somewhat strenuously, "*All are asleep—palaces, canals, people, / Only the spectre's gliding step...*"

He stared at Nikolai, expecting an answer.

"He's looking for a password," Dora's voice sounded in Nikolai's head. "Give me a second."

"And calm down, everything is under control," Mickey added.

Nikolai frowned, looking gravely into the distance over the stranger's shoulder.

"I found it," said Dora, "Repeat after me: *Only the head on the black platter / Looks longingly into the surrounding gloom.*"

When Nikolai had repeated the phrase, the stranger nodded with satisfaction and motioned for Nikolai to follow

---

[1] Alexander Blok, "A cold wind blows from the lagoon" (1909).

him. They approached the low archway, beyond which a narrow and dark alley led to the embankment. The stranger stopped, raised his hand, and listened.

"Toulemonde, behind you!" Mickey shouted. Turning around, Nikolai saw four black-clad figures toting machine guns.

A voice rang out from the darkness of the archway: "Don't move, you're surrounded!" A bearded old man armed with a pistol and accompanied by two machine gunners emerged into the pale light cast by the street lamp.

"You give me the backpack, the big guy puts the basket on the ground, we search you and go to the boat together," the old man ordered.

"On the count of three, you fall to the ground," Mickey commanded. "Three!"

Nikolai collapsed onto the stone pavement. Shots rang out from the far end of the square, and the four machine gunners fell. Meanwhile, the masked man threw a bottle of prosecco at the soldiers standing next to him. The bottle exploded in a fiery spray.

Engulfed in flame, the soldiers ran screaming down the dark tunnel to find watery salvation in the lagoon. Managing to dodge the explosion, the old man shot the masked man almost at point-blank range. The masked man crumpled to the ground. The old man ran up to Nikolai and tried to lift him to his feet. Several bullets flew past the old man. Swearing, General Loginov (it was him) dived into the darkness of the tunnel with incredible dexterity for his age.

Nikolai looked to the far side of the square, where Mickey and Dora stood in the dim light.

"Are you okay? He took off on a boat: I heard the sound of an engine," Mickey said.

"Yes," Nikolai answered faintly. "Help me!"

But Mickey and Dora silently retreated into the gloom.

"Turn around!" Nikolai heard Mickey whisper.

A few metres away from Nikolai, the tall man clambered to his feet, groaning. There was now a hole in his mask near the forehead, from which blood dripped to the ground. The man ran his hand over his cheek, causing the mask to turn red. "*Andiamo*," he muttered. Picking up the basket, he set off into the darkness.

"Go," said Dora. "That is your contact."

20

Passing through the low archway, they emerged on to the embankment. They heard shouts and footsteps behind them.

"Carabinieri! We'll take care of them, and you speed it up," Mickey said.

A light wind rose from the lagoon. On the island opposite stood a majestic monastery with four white classical columns and a tall brick belltower that looked as if it had sprung up from the dark water.

"*La chiesa di San Giorgio Maggiore,*" the Mask said proudly, wiping the blood from his eyes.

Shots rang out from the direction of the church.

After walking a couple of metres, Nikolai saw a moored boat in which a blond-haired young man sat drinking beer. He looked familiar. "Hello, Toulemonde!" he greeted Nikolai in Russian.

"Excuse me, but your friend," Nikolai shouted, "seems to be in bad shape."

"Who, Carlo?" The young man, surprised, looked at the mask, which was already crimson with blood. "Come on, it's only a scratch! Carlo is healthy as a bull and stubborn as a cockroach! Hurry up, your friends won't hold out for long. Give me the coin."

"The coin?" Vasiliev asked loudly, trying to shout over the noise of the gunshots.

"Yes, the one the girl gave you," the young man shouted back.

Nikolai fumbled in his pocket and took out the silver lira.

"Great! Welcome aboard," the young man said, smiling and looking at the coin.

Bleeding and tripping over the side, Carlo followed Nikolai into the boat.

As the boat pushed off, Nikolai gazed longingly at the Riva degli Schiavoni with its expensive hotels and luxurious mansions. The shooting stopped. It seemed to him that in the distance, in the darkness of the pier, something was moving.

"Were you expecting someone?" asked the young man, turning from the wheel.

"No, I'm just admiring Venice," Nikolai said, pulling himself together.

"It really is pretty. But don't look back, it's better to admire what's ahead!" advised the young man.

Cutting through the night, the boat moved towards the illuminated monastery. Reflected in the lagoon's calm waters against the starry sky, it resembled an art connoisseur's happy dream.

"So you don't remember Carlo and me?" the young man asked, shouting over the noise of the engine. "We met in Suren's Shop, when we were working part-time at a construction site. You signed a beer bottle for me, which I kept! My name is Andrei."

Nikolai stared at the young man. "I'm sorry, but how did you wind up here?" Nikolai asked, surprised.

Andrei glanced at Carlo. "Hey, go down below and clean yourself up. You'll get the boat dirty. And take off that mask finally!" Carlo grunted something and, bending over, slipped into the tiny cabin.

"How did you we wind up here?" Andrei paused. "We jumped into the Flow, and voila!" Andrei laughed.

When the boat was close to the monastery, Andrei turned off the engine.

"Carlo told me that a funny character once lived here, Father Pellegrino Ernetti, the man who invented the Chronovisor," Andrei said. "It transmits images and records sounds from the past. It's not an actual time machine, but more like a keyhole. Allegedly, everything that happens leaves behind a trace that can be restored. The Vatican confiscated the Chronovisor, just to be safe. It's a pity! Imagine, you could hear or see anyone, and maybe even ask them a question or ask them to forgive you."

Carlo, grunting, returned to the deck. He had thick black hair, tanned skin, and massive features—a long nose and a strong chin. An adhesive bandage was plastered to his forehead. He unhooked a large oar from the side of the boat and, standing on the stern, commenced rowing. At first the boat moved slowly, but Carlo's strength and skill were such that soon the San Giorgio Maggiore Monastery faded from view astern.

Fog had descended on the lagoon, and the illuminated wooden shoal warning markers poking out of the water were hardly legible. Carlo raised the oar, and the boat stopped. Nikolai looked quizzically at Andrei, who sat on a bench smoking.

"We are waiting for your friends and some old man. They can't go any further. I advise you to go to the bow," said Andrei, pulling out a pistol.

Carlo disappeared into the cabin and returned a minute later toting a heavy machine gun. Fitting it to the stern, he crouched down and aimed into the darkness. They sat in silence for a few minutes, listening to the water splashing and their own breathing. In the distance, the sound of a motor was heard, which suddenly stopped.

"*Adesso!*" Andrei commanded. The deafening roar of machine-gun fire ripped the silence to shreds and echoed across the lagoon.

Nikolai threw himself flat on his stomach, muffling his ears with his hands. After several endless seconds, Carlo stopped firing. The racket, after resounding back and forth across the lagoon a few times, finally subsided.

Nikolai sat up. Right then a motor began droning off to the side, quite close to the boat. He thought he glimpsed Mickey's red-cheeked face in the fog.

Andrei fired in the direction of the sound. Starting the boat, he surged forward before whipping around and exposing their pursuers to machine-gun fire. The abrupt turn nearly caused Carlo to drop the weapon rigged to the stern, but he was still able to squeeze off a burst into the fog.

The pursuers returned fire. Bullets whistled over Nikolai as he lay in the bow. Andrei continued to stand at the helm as if nothing was happening, paying no mind to the shooting. He pressed the gas, and the boat, rapidly accelerating, rushed with incredible speed, at some point barely touching the water. The shooting subsided, and the boat finally emerged from the fog.

Fighting down his fear, Nikolai got up the gumption to look aft.

He could barely make out the already distant figures of Mickey and Dora. Their bullet-riddled vessel was sinking. They stood holding each other up, gazing at Vasiliev flying away to parts unknown.

21

After a few minutes, the boat came to a stop. Andrei turned around and looked at the despondent Nikolai. "Your friends lucked out," Andrei said. "Carlo is a bad shot. He prefers swords."

"*Scimitarre*," Carlo clarified, descending into the cabin with the machine gun under his arm.

"But the old man has vanished. It doesn't matter though: he cannot get all the way out here," Andrei said. "I'm sorry, Toulemonde, but from here on out you are on your own. It's not far," he added.

"What do you mean, I'm on my own?" Nikolai asked anxiously.

"Hang on a second," Andrei said as he climbed onto the roof of the boat's cabin. "Carlo and I adore your movie. So, by way of farewell, we've decided to dedicate a poem to you."

Standing atop the cabin as if it were a stage, the young man recited:

Perhaps this is just a joke,
the witchery of cliffs and water.
A mirage? The traveller feels awful,
suddenly... no one, nothing?

He screamed, but no one heard him.
He tore away, fell
in the shaky pale distances
of Venetian mirrors.[2]

Nikolai backed up towards the stern.

"*Carlo, lo butta a mare,*"[3] Andrei commanded. Carlo abruptly grabbed Nikolai by the arm and pulled him towards himself. Nikolai swung at him with his free hand, but his fist got caught in Carlo's huge palm. Then Nikolai kicked the giant's knee with all his might. Carlo grunted in pain. Cursing, he grabbed Nikolai by the neck.

Andrei jumped onto the deck and, evincing remarkable strength, enveloped Nikolai in his arms. Snatching Nikolai, who was waving his arms and legs, out of Carlo's hands, Andrei dragged him to the side of the boat. Nikolai wriggled and pummelled Andrei's back, to no avail.

A moment later, Andrei threw the kicking Nikolai overboard. Waiting until he surfaced, Andrei tossed Nikolai his backpack. "Swim straight ahead or go back from where you came from, the choice is yours," he told Nikolai.

"Help me!" Nikolai shouted. "I don't know where to swim, I'm cold!"

"Swim that way," Andrei said, pointing off to one side. "You'll be in Venice in an hour. Fly out of here tomorrow morning and never come back. Or swim somewhere else."

"Where?" Nikolai yelled, floundering.

---

[2] Nikolai Gumilyov, "Venice" (1913), trans. Richard McKane.
[3] (Italian) "Carlo, throw him overboard."

"Wherever you want," said Andrei. Waving goodbye to Nikolai, he started the engine. The boat vanished into the darkness.

22

General Loginov had loved sports, especially swimming, since he was a child. Swimming across the lagoon was a snap for him. When the suspects threw Nikolai overboard, the general dived into the murky waters without hesitating. It was impossible keep up with the criminals' speedboat on his old vessel, but it was quite possible for the general to follow Nikolai. He was still in possession of the backpack containing the wooden case, so sooner or later someone would come for him. What was cruciak was not losing sight of Nikolai in the fog. Trying to maintain a distance, Loginov silently sliced through the lagoon's smooth canvas.

23

Spreading out his arms and legs, Nikolai looked up at the stars.

"What are we going to do?" Toulemonde asked. "It's chilly here, actually."

Nikolai rolled over on his stomach and, his arms raking up seaweed, swam.

The inner voice was agitated. "Where are you going? Venice is not this way."

Nikolai said nothing as he continued to swim in the pitch darkness.

Toulemonde rattled on. "Listen, shit happens. Let's go back to land, think it over, and regroup…"

Nikolai was not listening. The annoying Toulemonde shut up after a while. An uncustomary, sweet silence was restored in Nikolai's head: the inner voices had gone to ground, Mickey and Dora showed no signs of life, and the advertising worms had long since evaporated.

Nikolai flipped over on his back again and, savouring the solitude, stared at a sky in which millions of stars winked at each other and chatted. Fortunately, they were so far away that their eternal conversations did not disturb Venetian Lagoon's blessed peace.

In a few minutes, Nikolai was frozen stiff. His hair, face, and clothes were encrusted with a brownish-green algae, and his arms resembled green wings. The seaweed felt soft and warm, like a fluffed feather bed, and Nikolai wanted to immerse himself in it. Since he had no advisers left and there was no one to reason with him, this was exactly what he did. Stretching out as if he were standing at attention, he squeezed his eyes shut and let himself sink to the muddy bottom.

When, a few seconds later, his eyes had grown accustomed to the murky water, Nikolai peered through the underwater vines and spotted a woman's remains lying on a bed of marine plants. Her wet grey hair barely covered her yellowish skull, the skin on her face had slid off to one side, and her mouth was twisted in a semblance of a smile. A soft light radiated from the empty eye sockets—phosphorescent algae were most likely growing in them or a mollusc had set up house. A white jacket enveloped the shrunken body. Pushing through the thick algae, Nikolai lay down next to the woman and placed his head on her chest, which steadily rose and fell. Nikolai felt warm. Tears welled up in his eyes, immediately dissolving in the turbid water.

Nikolai recalled the fateful day. Vera had come home late. Inebriated as usual, he was sprawled on the bed, horns clamped to his temples. In his mind, he was brilliantly performing the starring role in a movie. Vera yanked off the horns, which was dangerous because returning suddenly from the Flow was tantamount to surfacing from a great depth too rapidly. In the event, Nikolai got off with a bad case of dizziness and nausea. Vera screamed for a long time and even tried to hit Nikolai. He had kept his cool, however, knowing that Vera loved him, no matter how drunk, filthy, and stupid he was—and that, in any case, he absolutely had to dive back into the Flow as soon as possible. Nikolai patiently waited for his wife to shut up and go to bed or, even better, to run off to her mother's house. After screaming for half an hour, Vera finally burst into tears, slammed the door, and bolted from of the house. Nikolai sighed and donned the horns, resuming his film. It had probably been *Casablanca*, he thought. *Here's looking at you, kid.* Rick Blaine smiled, gazing at the love of his life, pledged to another man. It had occurred to Nikolai then that he would have played the scene better than Bogart had.

The next day brought sirens, police, robot detectives, questioning, documents, phone calls from Vera's mother. It was an open-and-shut case: drugs, the lake, death. No one else was to blame for anything.

"Come on, Vera, let's go!" Nikolai pleaded, crying. He gently lifted the shrivelled body into his arms and, pushing off from the soft bottom, swam up towards the surface. They rose above the underwater forest. Nikolai felt that things were finally good between them.

"It's just a little farther," Nikolai whispered, hugging the bones. The water brightened, salvation was near. But Vera was fragile: why had he not understood this before? The bones fell apart and, turning into dust, sank back down into the mud. Crying, Nikolai emerged from the water alone.

24

Wiping tears and snot from his face, Nikolai floated aimlessly in the lagoon. A boat or a big snag emerged from the fog. No! It was the bed, so soft and comfortable, in which he and Vera had slept. The gentle current nudged the bed towards Nikolai. He grabbed the headboard with the last of his strength and, fouling the snow-white sheet with algae, curled up under the blanket. Feeling warm and cosy, Nikolai closed his eyes.

Nikolai was about to fall asleep when someone ripped the blanket off him. He was blinded by a bright light. A second later, he saw the orderly's face, blood oozing from his mutilated eye socket. Grabbing Nikolai with an icy hand, the orderly tried to pull him off the bed. "It's time for your treatment," the orderly wheezed, but Nikolai did not want to go for treatment. He yelled and kicked. Miraculously freeing himself, he leapt from the bed.

The floor turned out to be the water of the lagoon, and Nikolai immediately sank to the bottom. It was not a deep spot, though. Vasiliev stood up to his neck in cold water and fetid algae, but he was finally free.

The fog sketched Vera's face, which smiled compassionately at Nikolai. He smiled back gratefully. He felt that he had been forgiven. Women were privy to the sorrowful wisdom, which was their true punishment, that sooner or later the life they brought into the world, the love they nurtured, and the beauty they tried to preserve would all dissolve into stagnation, like a pinch of salt in the cosmic broth that slightly affected its flavour, at best. It was their sense of pity and there realisation of life's fragility that made women stand by negligent husbands, raise the bawling next generation, and tend to dying old people. Some, like Vera, could not cope with it, but they always forgave, always.

Nikolai took a few cautious steps, afraid to fall into deep water, but the shoal rose higher, so that in a few minutes the water was knee-deep.

Shivering from the cold, Nikolai pushed forward, watching his feet and squishing his boots in the mud. A cool breeze blew, causing goosebumps to crawl over his body. The wind carried voices to his location. Raising his head, he saw a yellowish point of lamplight in the distance. He stopped. He did not want to interrupt his solitude by talkint to people and answering questions. But there was nothing to be done about it: his body needed warmth. Sighing, Nikolai walked towards the light. After taking a couple of steps, he suddenly plunged into deep water. Surfacing and barely regaining his breath, he paddled desperately towards the light.

A few minutes later, a dock emerged from the darkness. Andrei and Carlo sat playing dice at a folding table under a streetlight. They paid no attention to Nikolai as he swam up.

"Help me!"croaked Nikolai.

Andrei tore himself away from the game and, looking at Nikolai, shouted, "You've got it all mixed up—Venice is that way!" Andrei gestured into the darkness. Then he looked at Carlo and whispered in Italian, "You owe me a denarius." Carlo shrugged and resumed playing.

Nikolai barely swam to the pier. He climbed up a metal ladder and sat down in an empty chair at the gaming table.

"You sure you don't want to go back?" Andrei asked after throwing the dice. "Carlo and I can do it in a jiffy—"

"I don't," Nikolai said, cutting him off.

"Do you want to play?"

"No. Do you happen to have any clothes?"

"We do happen to have some." Andrei pointed to the boat. "Look in there and take a shower while you're at it, while we finish our game."

Nikolai trudged to the boat. To his surprise, he found a black suit, a snow-white shirt, leather shoes, a belt, underwear, and a towel in the cabin. The clothes were the right size. After washing up and changing, he felt a surge of energy. Returning briskly to the pier, he found that the game table was folded, and his backpack was on the ground, with Andrei and Carlo standing on either side of it.

"You look great," Andrei said.

Carlo agreed. "*Bene, bene.*"

"Come on, I'll show you the way," said Andrei. "It's close, but it's easy to get lost. And the area is swampy."

Looking around, Nikolai saw an dilapidated oblong building covered in scaffolding not far from the pier. He could make out the outline of a slightly leaning bell tower beyond it. Except for the splashing of water and the rustling of leaves, the island was perfectly quiet.

"Here's another curious spot," Andrei said, catching Nikolai's eye. "Plague victims were brought here in the Middle Ages. They say two hundred thousand died here, although the island is tiny… In the early twentieth century, that building," Andrei motioned towards the ruins, "housed an experimental psychiatric hospital run by a notorious doctor. He experimented on people. One day, the patients rebelled and tossed him off the bell tower. Or maybe he jumped. There was a heavy fog that day. Legend has it that many people saw the doctor's body flying from the bell tower, but no one could tell whether it fell to the ground or disappeared into the fog. In any case, the body was never found… Okay, let's go."

Carlo tapped Nikolai on the shoulder and, returning to the boat, sat down in the stern. Andrei continued his story.

"There were many attempts to clean up the island, but they all failed." They turned into a grove. "Superstitious Italians sometimes saw ghosts or heard sighs in the darkness."

"Where are we going?" Nikolai asked, interrupting him. "Isn't the building over there?"

"That's the old hospital, but the laboratory is beyond the woods. Come on, Toulemonde, don't be afraid. There are no ghosts here!" Looking at Nikolai's pale face, Andrei grinned.

"What kind of laboratory?" asked Nikolai.

"It's a whim of our boss. He is rich and loves science. It's his idea of fun."

They wandered in the dark among densely packed trees, tripping over the roots every now and then. There were abandoned buildings all around them. At last they came to a clearing. The full moon appeared from behind the clouds. Nikolai noticed a swaying wall on the other side of the clearing.

"That is a reed grove," said Andrei. "It has grown wild. Come on, we don't have much time."

The reeds were so tall and dense that they barely admitted the moonlight. Andrei deftly crawled between the green trunks, guiding Nikolai deeper and deeper into the grove. He stumbled and the leaves whipped his face, threatening to poke him now in the eye, now in the nose.

"Didn't you say that the island is small?" Nikolai asked after an hour of battling the annoying reeds.

"It is small, but it's a long walk," Andrei muttered. "Stop!" he exclaimed, raising his hand. "Do you hear that?"

It seemed to Nikolai that through the rustling of the leaves he heard the voice of an animal. He was surprised. "What is it?"

"A cow," Andrei replied. "And where there are cows, there are people. It's a good thing, because I was starting to worry that we were lost."

Turning back around, Andrei followed the sound. After a quarter of an hour, the reeds gave way first to small bushes, and then to large trees—birches and pines.

"We're almost there," Andrei said with relief.

They came out of the woods onto a road. In the distance, Nikolai saw a small building illuminated by white light.

"That's our destination," said Andrei.

Looking higher up, Nikolai noticed flickering red lights.

"Is that a windmill?" he asked, surprised.

"Yes, it is. Our pride and joy."

Hastening his pace, Nikolai headed for the building. Then he started running. Out of breath, he stopped next to the closed door.

"Do you recognise it?" Andrei asked, catching up with him.

A illuminated sign hung above the entrance to the building: *Suren's Shop—Open 24/7.*

Nikolai looked back at Andrei, apparently expecting an explanation, but Andrei only shrugged his shoulders. "It's time for me to go back," he said. Before Nikolai could ask him anything, Andrei had turned around and quickly set off back towards the forest.

25

Nikolai stood staring at the shop's front door of the shop. The wind whipped up. The blades of the wind turbine began to move, producing the familiar drone.

"What should I do?" Nikolai asked aloud. The voices in his head were silent. He looked around: there was not another soul in sight. Yellow leaves fell on the pavement, wet from the recent rain.

Nikolai checked his phone: it was three o'clock in the morning. He was dog-tired, and his legs felt like cotton wool. He swayed and fell awkwardly on one knee on the pavement. Something clinked in his left hand: he was holding a plastic bag. Laboriously, he stood up, brushing a soggy yellow leaf from his knee. He opened the bag and saw two empty vodka bottles in it. His head spun and ached at the same time—a sure sign of alcohol withdrawal. He dragged himself to the stairs at the entrance to the shop and sat down. He tried to reconstruct the events of the previous evening.

He remembered that, after getting the bottle of vodka from Suren, he had gone home. He had planned a nice evening on the horns, but suddenly the phone had rung. After that, he drank a little more than usual, either for joy or out of grief. Then everything had kicked off: the National Hotel, his dead wife, Venice... But now, for some reason, he again found himself at Suren's Shop.

Nikolai looked at the bag. It dawned on him that he had come to the shop to turn in the bottles and buy beer with the proceeds. He decided that beer would really hit the spot right then.

Approaching the steel door, he pressed the doorbell. Suren always locked the store at night. After a couple of minutes, Nikolai heard the sounds of footsteps. A familiar, almost kindred voice croaked, "I'm coming, I'm coming." The lock clicked, the door opened, and Nikolai saw the shopkeeper's drowsy face in the doorway.

"Hi, Suren," Nikolai mumbled, staring at the floor.

"Hello, Kolya, come in," Suren replied.

Nikolai noticed that, despite his sleepy appearance, Suren was dressed to the nines, as always, in a snow-white shirt and black trousers.

Going behind the highly polished counter, Suren asked, "What do you want? Don't tell me. I know what a man needs at this time of the night." He set a bottle of beer on the counter. "It's probably none of my business, but it's time for you to go cold turkey. You're killing yourself."

"I remembered Vera, and that is..." Nikolai said without looking up.

"I see... Go home, go to bed. And get her out of your head."

"I don't understand what's going on, Suren. I think I'm going crazy," Nikolai said, his voice faltering.

Suren stood back from the counter and, striking a pose, solemnly recited: "I loved you. Love (maybe / it's mere pain) still drills my brains. / Everything is smashed to smithereens."[4]

"Ugh, more poems! My head aches as it is!" Nikolai pleaded.

"Drink the beer and you'll feel better." Suren was miffed. "I like to recite poetry while I'm waiting for clients."

Opening the bottle, Nikolai took a couple of sips.

"You're a good fellow, Kolya, a genuine human being. There are almost no people like you nowadays."

Nikolai set the bottle on the counter, looking at Suren with surprise. His manner of speaking had changed a great deal: his Armenian accent had vanished.

"People have lost their way," Suren continued. "They've forgotten how to really feel. They've stopped being interesting even to *Him*." Suren pointed up. "They implant hardware in their heads. They fall in love less and less often. They don't really want anything and they're not afraid."

Nikolai's head had stopped hurting. "Suren, aren't you Armenian?"

"Armenian, Armenian," Suren answered absent-mindedly and continued. "Frankly speaking, Kolya, you're no intellectual. You're not terribly observant and you have nasty habits. But you are dearer to me than anyone else. How you trembled with fear when the plane took off! How you wept with delight when you caught sight of Venice! How you repented when you encountered Vera! It's worth fighting for your soul because your energy is pure."

---

[4] Joseph Brodsky, "I Loved You" (1974).

"I don't really understand what you're talking about. What happened to your accent? Who are you anyway?" Nikolai asked excitedly.

"Don't sweat it. You were warned to be ready for anything. I am the one to whom the goods must be delivered. If you feel more comfortable, I can go back to doing the accent: I'm just tired of it. And I'm tired of standing at this counter. Let's go to the back room, sit down at the table, and talk like normal people while we wait."

Suren pushed the black door, which creaked open.

"Who are we waiting for?" Nikolai asked.

"The clients," Suren replied. After letting Nikolai into the back room, the shopkeeper slammed the door shut.

<h1 style="text-align:center">26</h1>

The walls of the back room were lined with shelves, on which canned food and bottles of alcohol stood in neat rows. In the centre of the small clean room Nikolai saw a round wooden table and four chairs. There was an ancient black phone with a round dial on the table.

Suren motioned for Nikolai to sit down, and he settled himself in the chair next to Nikolai.

"I'm sorry, but I wasn't able to deliver the package to your cousin," Nikolai said.

"It doesn't matter," Suren said, brushing aside his apology. "What matters is that you're here."

"Why?" Nikolai was surprised.

"Because the package is you," Suren said mysteriously. With a predatory glint in his eyes, he continued. "We need to talk about Vera."

Nikolai had not gone to her funeral. But he often dreamed about a funeral service in an empty old church, where she lay in a wooden coffin among yellow and white flowers. She was seemingly alive. In the dim light, the eyelashes moved, the chest heaved slightly.

Vera opened her eyes. Leaning against the sides of the narrow coffin, she struggled to stand up. A light fog shrouded the church. The coffin resembled a boat sailing into the haze.

Vera looked at Nikolai and tried to tell him something, but couldn't get the words out. The fog thickened, the candles hissed out one by one. The lights on the wind turbine flickered, casting bloody light on the dead woman's white face. She held out a bony hand to Nikolai.

Nikolai grabbed his head. The image of the dead woman standing in the coffin disappeared into the fog. He heard water splashing and felt soft, slimy algae on his feet. A shiver ran through his body, and he floundered in the icy water. A lantern flashed far ahead in the fog. Nikolai shuddered and saw Suren's face before him.

"She has forgiven me," Nikolai whispered.

"She has, but I haven't," Suren replied, grinning.

Nikolai wanted to get up, but he was not able to get up. An uncanny force pinned him to the chair.

The phone rang. Suren picked it up, irritated.

"*Pronto!* Loginov? Okay, bring him in."

The door creaked open, and Carlo entered the room, leading an old man who was trying to resist by the hand. "He followed us all the way from Venice. And then, you know, there's his age," Carlo reported in Italian.

"So, Pyotr Vasilyevich, your little heart couldn't take it and you had to do everything yourself," Suren purred, looking at Loginov. "Attention!" Suren suddenly shouted in a thunderous bass, forcing the old man to stand at attention. "Good, good," Suren muttered, looking into his pocket mirror. "Do you recognise him?" the shopkeeper asked, pointing at Nikolai.

"Yes, sir!" Loginov rapped out.

"At ease," Suren commanded. "Is his access to the AI after his wife's death your doing?"

"Not at all," Logvinov replied. "But I—"

"That's enough. Let's see," Suren interrupted and, thinking for a second, continued. "Pyotr Vasilyevich Loginov. FSB officer, champion of Russian national greatness, two hundred people killed, five thousand lives mutilated, plus another one now. His beloved dog is called Fairy. I'm impressed by your enthusiasm, but your ambitions are groundless. You fancy yourself the demiurge of history, but you're actually a boring piece of shit. You were right to dislike your mother, however. Do you know what she did with the money she got when her husband was killed? She secretly donated it to rape victims in Ukraine! Do you know why she did it?"

Loginov looked dumbfounded at Suren as he went on.

"Because she knew perfectly well how painful it was when those big, strong hands you remember so fondly punched her in the face or some other part of her body. By the way, your father and his friends had loads of fun in Ukraine: they raped, they murdered, they pillaged. Well done, a real liberator! But he died like a dog while shitting in a trench. What about you? You've been sitting on your ass all your life, you haven't done anything worthwhile. So, farewell. Take him to the third floor, Carlo, and dispatch Fairy to the slaughterhouse."

"Permission to speak freely!" Logvinov shouted hoarsely.

"Permission denied," Suren replied, yawning.

There was a tiny elevator in a dark corner of the backroom. Carlo dragged the reluctant Loginov into the elevator's dimly lit car.

"Spare me! They'll exchange me for someone good," the old man shouted.

After shoving Loginov into the elevator, Carlo deftly pressed the button. The doors instantly closed, and the cabin plunged into the abyss.

"Forward, Russia!" the old man managed to shout as he sped off into the underworld.

"*Grazie*, Carlo! Don't touch the dog," Suren purred contentedly.

The tall Italian nodded and, winking at Nikolai, left the room.

"So, where were we? Yes, you killed Vera. You ignored her wishes, suffocated her with your authority, and squashed her creative side. By the way, she could have become a famous art critic, run seminars on contemporary art, and written a book about that—what's its name?—Pi Yang. But Vera met you, to her sorrow, and your indifference and narcissism smashed all her hopes and dreams to smithereens. That is how it was. And that is why your soul belongs to me."

"I didn't kill her," Nikolai pleaded.

"You killed her, you killed her. Well, the heck with it. You lucked out because I need you. I have a plan. Everyone sees clearing that the world is falling into the abyss. Nobody knows what to do. But I know! Humanity must be brought out of its intellectual coma, given drugs through a dropper, spoonfed potions, and only then served delicious dishes," Suren continued pompously, examining his hair in a pocket mirror. "So first we shall revive the cinema. Then we will reteach people to have a feel for painting, literature, poetry, and all the rest. You have to start somewhere, don't you? You can't immediately show them Tiepolo, force them to listen to Mahler, or to read Brodsky, can you? We'll start with a simple but well-made action movie featuring an emphatically positive hero, and then we'll see. You'll be the star. How do you like that?"

Vasiliev didn't know how to respond.

"People have become extremely dull, there is no one to talk to. Their souls have lost texture and taste. That stupid Flow is to blame for everything. We will destroy it, reopen the cinemas, and start making movies. You will do what you love, become famous again, earn a lot of money. Not to mention the women: your Vera is a dog compared to the women you'll have. Although, I'm sorry, she's certainly pretty too. People will go for you: you've got that something special. Carlo and Andrei agree with me."

"And then?" Nikolai asked.

"And then? You mean after death?"

"And then it's the elevator for you. You'll go downstairs in any case, because Vera's death is on your conscience. Besides, you're a murderer, a drunk, and a crook. As part of a state-run criminal gang, you stole proprietary technologies. And, just yesterday, you sold drugs to minors, and the day before yesterday you stuck a syringe in the eye of a poor nurse. So you're going into the elevator however you slice it, either now or after numerous years of fame and success. As an additional encouragement, I promise to send you to the first floor with the philosophers, scientists, and artists. But if you don't agree to my terms, you'll go down to the floor with the murderers, like Loginov. Do we have a deal?"

"I don't know," stammered Nikolai, glancing at the door. Suren had clearly gone mad, fancying himself Lucifer, a philosopher and, worst of all, a film producer. Hypertrophied narcissism and megalomania had clouded his mind.

"I agree to everything, or else I'll end up in the basement, like poor old Loginov."

"Perfect!" Suren beamed. "We'll sign the contract later, but in the meantime, let's go downstairs. I'll show you how everything works. On the minus ground floor, where you'll be living, there are wonderful labs, film studios, and workshops staffed by the smartest, talented people. You'll be thrilled!"

"Maybe later?" bleated Nikolai.

"No, now," Suren insisted, getting up from his chair. "You're afraid, but your whole being craves creative success, fame, and money. I can feel it."

Either the back room had shrunk, or the puny Armenian had become two heads taller, but Suren suddenly seemed like a giant to Nikolai. Rubbing his eyes, he found himself standing at the open doors of the elevator. Holding him by the elbow, Suren, already his usual size, gently pushed him forward.

"Come on, it'll be a quick trip, there and back."

"No!" Vasiliev resisted, but Suren pushed him into the elevator and, squeezing in behind him, nimbly pressed the button marked "-1". The elevator doors began to close. Desperately struggling with Suren, Nikolai stuck out his foot. Instead of stopping, however, the doors clamped down hard on his foot and Nikolai screamed in pain. Pushing Suren aside, he clung to the doors with his hands, trying in vain to pry them open, while Suren, grabbing him by the waist, tried to drag him back into the elevator.

The phone on the table suddenly rang.

"Damn it," Suren muttered, pressing the "stop" button. "Let me through," he added in a businesslike tone. He pushed aside Nikolai, who moaned in pain.

Suren ran to the phone and picked up the receiver.

"What is it now? Ah… Well, let him in," he said irritably.

Taking advantage of the timeout, Nikolai limped towards the door. Although the back room was small, there was no way he could make it to the door: although he ran and ran, he seemed to be standing still. Desperate, Nikolai jumped forward, grabbed the door handle, and pulled with all his might. The door creaked open. Nikolai dashed out of the store, hitting his head painfully on the door jamb. Fortunately, there was no one outside.

27

At the end of the working day, Stavarsky wearily plopped down in the upholstered chair in his home cinema. Filming was underway: the actors were putting in decent performances, the special effects were top flight, and the plot was a roller coast. And yet something was off. Perhaps Toulemonde was not playing his role well enough, but due to certain obligations Stavarsky could not replace him. Besides, he was worried that his cutting-edge picture, whose highlight was the interweaving of the director's fantasies with the protagonist's imagination, had devolved into pure improvisation. The film was out of control: the plot was writing itself, and there was no telling how the thing would end. As a scientist, Stavarsky was glad to have the chance to observe this curious phenomenon, but as a director, he did not want to give his brainchild free rein. Tomorrow he would put everything in its place by making a surprise cameo appearance in his own film, as Hitchcock, Scorsese, Tarantino, Kitano, Polanski, Ryazanov, and many other auteurs of the old-time cinema had done.

But that was tomorrow. Today, Stavarsky had poured himself a whiskey and settled down to watch a simple but masterfully shot film featuring courageous, fearless heroes. It was a western entitled *Butch Cassidy and the Sundance Kid,* the story of two cowboys, knights of a vanishing era, who were doomed to die. The lights in the room went out. Stavarsky closed his eyes and, hearing the 20th Century Fox fanfare, savoured his first sip. As the story unfolded, Stavarsky felt a sweet sadness as he sipped the whiskey and whispered Butch and Sundance's lines. The world of cowboys was a legend, of course. The Wild West had been a dangerous place, but it had not been even remotely as cruel and unscrupulous as the world of today, if only because in those distant days there had been no internet, cerebral worms, or atomic bombs.

Nowadays, you couldn't stop trains to rob them, because modern locomotives raced through concrete tunnels at supersonic speeds. You couldn't blow up a safe to get at the gold and banknotes inside it: such things now could be seen only in museums. Love wouldn't make you suffer because feelings had gone out of fashion. Back in the their day, cowboys could escape from justice by fleeing to Mexico or Uruguay, but where could you hide from the all-seeing Flow?

And yet the world was a better place. Stavarsky blinked, and a cowboy hat appeared on his head, and a revolver materialised in his free hand. The tragic finale approached. The cornered cowboys dashed out of their final refuge to face certain death. Shots were fired. Stavarsky also shot from a digital revolver. There were no cowboys anymore. They were not of this world.

"Not of this world," Stavarsky purred.

Many narrow-minded people did not understand the simple rule that the past must make way for the future. Logvinov, a relic of a bygone era, was already buried on the minus third floor of Suren's Shop. Soon there would be no more retrogrades trying to stop the coming revolution.

28

The wind blew, the turbine hummed low notes, and the red warning lights cut through the darkness. Looking around for pursuers and limping, Nikolai ran towards his house. No one was in pursuit.

The humming split his head, the bright flashes of red light made his eyes water, and his elevator-assaulted foot throbbed. Trying to ignore the unpleasant sensations, Nikolai finally got to his dacha. Out of the darkness floated the spidery old apple trees that concealed his tiny house. Hands trembling, Nikolai reached into his pocket, found the key, opened the door. He locked the door from the inside after he entered the house, leaving behind the windmill's drone and the blinding flicker of the red lights.

Nikolai checked all the rooms: no one was there. Then he barricaded the front door with a heavy nightstand, grabbed knives from the kitchen, and locked himself in the bedroom. After laboriously blocking the door with the wardrobe, he phoned the police.

The on-duty bot reacted to the phrase "I'm being chased by a serial killer": a patrol unit would arrive in five minutes. Sitting on the bed, Nikolai threw off his shoe with relief: his foot was swollen, the skin had taken on a bluish hue. Nikolai stretched out on the soft mattress and listened. The wind had died down, the rain dripped on the roof. The phone rang.

"Mr. Vasilyev? It's the police: we're outside your house. Are you okay?"

Nikolai looked out of the window. In the darkness he saw the gleam of two flashlights.

"Yes," Nikolai replied. "Send me your ID." The algorithm confirmed its authenticity. Nikolai was relieved. "I'm opening the door."

After laboriously removing the barricades he had erected a few minutes earlier, Nikolai opened the front door. The bright light made him squint. When his eyes got used to it, he discovered that the apple orchard was gone, and a long lighted corridor had replaced his yard. Doors opened and closed, people hurrying in and out of them.

"Damn it!" Nikolai swore and, returning inside, slammed the door behind him. "I'm tired, I'm not going anywhere. I'm tired!"

There was a knock on the door.

"Go away!" yelled Nikolai.

A pleasant female voice was heard from behind the door. "Nikolai Vasilyevich, please report to makeup, everything is ready."

"I told you to go to hell!" Nikolai blurted out. After thinking for a second, he repeated the voice's request as a question. "To makeup?"

"Yes, Nikolai Vasilyevich, the crew is waiting, and Scandalous is concerned."

"Does that mean we're shooting?" Nikolai laughed. "Well played. And what, exactly, are we shooting?"

"*Agent Toulemonde 2: From Light to Darkness and Back*, Nikolai Vasilyevich! What else?" the voice replied in surprise.

Nikolai slumped down the wall to the floor. Of course: the sequel to the movie that had made him famous. Filming had never commenced due to the war. After the war ended in defeat, people no longer had a need for that film in particular or cinema in general.

"Very cute, you've persuaded me," Nikolai conceded. He got up and opened the door.

"My god!" exclaimed the pretty girl, her eyes wide open. "Nikolai Vasilyevich, come quickly, you need to—"

"Shed twenty years and lose ten kilograms," Nikolai finished her sentence.

"God forbid! You just need to freshen up a little," the girl chirped, guiding Nikolai down the corridor.

As if in a dream, Nikolai followed the girl, nodding to the people passing them. They came to a door marked *Toulemonde*. Inside was a spacious dressing room with a large mirror, a TV, and a bar. As soon as Nikolai entered the room, a young man with multicoloured hair rushed up to him.

"Nicolas, are you crazy?" the young man shouted in despair. "Look at you—you're all puffy! And your hair! Dear god! When did you go grey? Sit down quickly! Tell Scandalous that Nicolas will be ready in two hours, no earlier," the young man commanded the girl.

"Fine," the girl replied. "Would you like anything, Nikolai Vasilyevich?"

"Yes, water and a copy of the script," Nikolai demanded. "What scene are we shooting?"

The young man and the girl traded glances.

"The fight scene with McDee," the girl answered, dashing out of the room.

"How was your weekend?" the young man asked after seating Nikolai in an armchair. Without waiting for an answer, the makeup artist rattled on.

"Mine was terrible. We went to Seryozha's parents. His dad still doesn't know about us. He asked whether we were classmates at uni. Can you imagine? And yet, he was wearing red sweater with a Christmas tree. His mom played the fool all evening, and she did a great job of it. Can you imagine, at the most crucial moment, when I was talking about work, Seryozha put his hand on my knee and squeezed it so hard! I spilled my glass right on Dad's sweater, and he—"

"Hang on," Nikolai interrupted. "What do Seryozha's folks call you?"

"What do they call me? They call me by my name, what else?" The young man was surprised.

Nikolai was insistent. "Answer the question."

"You really are crazy—Yura, of course!"

"I see," said Nikolai. "You have to forgive me, Yura. I got a good buzz on this weekend, and my memory is whacked."

"Yeah, I get it," Yura said good-naturedly, combing Nikolai's hair. "Now we'll touch up the highlights a bit and rub in some cream, and you'll be as good as new."

Footsteps and screams were audible outside the door before a middle-aged man burst into the dressing room. The young female assistant stood dejectedly behind him.

29

Nikolai opened his mouth in surprise when he saw the newcomer. He knew this man.

"Nikolai!" Stavarsky said in a menacing voice, while winking slightly at Nikolai. "You know how much each day of shooting costs! You promised not to drink! I, the world-renowned film director Yakov Stavarsky aka Scandalous cannot afford to get off schedule! I get it—the New Year, the holidays—but Kolya, I implore you to pull it together!"

"But there's no movie without me, without Toulemonde," Nikolai said, playing his role. "Basically, there's nothing without me. So, give me the script, Yasha, because I've forgotten half my lines, and make yourself scarce. I'll be ready in three hours."

"Why you…" Stavarsky could not seem to find the right words. Finally, he continued. "I've given Petrova and Sinitsyn the heads-up. They're upset, but they'll wait for you. Here's the script." He snatched a sheaf of paper from the assistant standing behind him. "Today's scene is highlighted in yellow," said Stavarsky, flinging the script on the dressing room table. Then, looking at Nikolai, he winked again. "And suck in your gut: you're supposed to be a superhero!"

"It serves him right," said Yura when the dressing room door had closed. "He thinks he's a great director? If it weren't for you—"

"Leave me in peace," Nikolai blurted out angrily as he immersed himself in the script.

The setting is a post-apocalyptic world. Our protagonist is Nikolai Vasilyev, a lonely old actor with a split personality or a severe personality disorder. In reality, he is Toulemonde, a spy in a secret program run by the Artificial Intelligence Research Institute. His memories have been erased and replaced with fictional events. His antagonist is a crazed fan of cutting-edge technology. Using Vasilyev as his pawn, he launches a super-sophisticated AI which has previously been housed in a virtual universe into the real world. Although we first see Toulemonde as a weakling and a bore, he gradually re-emerges as the hero he once was decades ago. A fateful showdown is in the offing...

This introduction was followed by blank lines highlighted in yellow marker.

"And where is the rest?" Nikolai was surprised.

"Haha, very funny," Yura replied sarcastically.

"I'm not joking," said Nikolai, lifting his eyes from the page.

"Well, this is the new fad—real virtuality. Scandalous devised it. It's all the rage in cinema. Scenes are shot in order, but there is a lot of improvisation, special effects, and all that. Only the shot footage goes into the script. The rest is added as the drama unfolds, so to speak. Then they do a lot of editing. You see?"

"I get it, I guess…" Nikolai scratched his head.

A few hours later, a rejuvenated Nikolai was trying to pour himself into a skinny pair of Levi's when the door swung open and Stavarsky flew into the dressing room.

"Kolya, this is unbearable! Petrova is headed back to the hotel, and Sinitsyn telephoned his lawyer. It's now or never!" Stavarsky said, his voice cracking.

"I'll be right there," Nikolai puffed, barely able to button his jeans. "Could you just explain to me what's going on?"

Stavarsky threw up his hands. "There is a big movie going on, my friend! Come on, it's time to shoot it!"

A few minutes later they entered the studio, which contained nothing but white walls, a strange-looking piece of equipment apparently used for filming, a man who looked uncannily like Mickey, and a woman who resembled Dora.

"Fucking finally!" Mickey's double exclaimed.

"This is an outrage, Vasilyev! I get it, but you're not the only one working here. I have a husband, children, and a lover, after all!" said Dora's double as she walked up to Nikolai. She kissed him on the cheek and whispered into his ear, "Lay off the sweets, you've gone to fat."

"Attention, please!" Stavarsky shouted into a megaphone. "We're filming the fight scene. The first take is the final take. Action!"

30

Blinded by the flashlights, Vasiliev realised he had made a mistake. He stood face to face with Andrei and Carlo, dressed in police uniforms.

"You're such a naïve dude," said Andrei.

"*Idioto*," Carlo concurred, adjusting the band-aid on the bridge of his nose.

Without thinking twice, Nikolai charged off the porch towards Andrei, who stood a couple of steps below him, and kicked him in the head. Andrei fell backwards into an apple tree and, colliding with the trunk, collapsed to the ground. Carlo grabbed Nikolai, lifted him into the air, and smashed him down on the pavement with all his might. Sparks flew in Nikolai's eyes. Focusing his gaze, he saw Carlo looming over him. Apparently cursing in Italian, Carlo was taking a rope from his pocket when a red dot appeared on his forehead near the band-aid. Carlo uttered a long curse, after which he jerked and collapsed on his back like a felled tree. Dora jumped out of the bushes with a sniper rifle at the ready. Wielding a flamethrower with a burning fuse, Mickey ran out behind her.

"Sorry, this might harm the apple trees," Mickey said, dousing the prone Andrei and Carlo in flame.

"What are you doing!" Nikolai yelled.

"This will delay them. Let's run!" Dora shouted back by way of an answer.

Nikolai looked at Andrei and Carlo's motionless burning bodies, cast a glance in the direction of his cosy house, and ran towards the gate.

31

Throwing the weapons into the trunk, Mickey jumped behind the wheel. Dora got into the back seat, while Nikolai got into the front seat.

"It's close," Mickey said hopefully.

The car shot up into the sky and landed at Suren's Shop a few seconds later.

"Why did we have to come here?" Nikolai exclaimed, surprised.

"To talk," Mickey said. He turned the car sideways to the store's entrance. "Hide behind the car. There's a pistol in the glove compartment," he commanded.

When the trio had settled behind the car, Mickey shouted loudly, "Suren, come out, we need to talk!"

Silence ensued.

Nikolai's short time on the movie set had gone to his head, apparently. He was tired of standing on the sidelines. It was his Flow, his movie, his life, after all.

"What are you waiting for? After me!" he boldly exclaimed. Clutching the pistol, he advanced on the store, expecting the others to follow him single file.

"Wait!" Dora shouted. Rushing at Nikolai, she knocked him over. A shot rang out from behind the trees. Dora screamed: a bullet had clipped her in the shoulder.

"Damn it!" Mickey exclaimed. Taking a pistol from his pocket, he fired several shots towards the trees, then lifted Dora and laboriously set her down against the wheel of the car. Although Dora was breathing, she was unconscious. Blood oozed from her wound. Mickey pulled a bandage from his pocket and dressed the injured shoulder snugly.

"She won't last long, she needs medication. We have to make a dash for the store. Are you ready?" Mickey asked.

Nikolai glanced at Dora's face, white as snow, then turned his gaze to the frowning Mickey.

"Like Butch Cassidy and the Sundance Kid?" Nikolai asked suddenly.

"Something like that," said Mickey, grinning. "On the count of three, I go right, you go left. As soon as you step out, shoot anywhere but at me. Understood?"

"Yeah."

"You're not such a coward, after all," Mickey said approvingly. Taking a deep breath, he shouted, "Three!"

Firing into the air, Nikolai ran screaming towards the store. Shots rang out. Something pummelled him in the chest and leg. He fell.

I'm a goner, Nikolai thought, closing his eyes.

The shooting stopped. The leaves rustled pleasantly, and rain dripped on Nikolai's face. He opened his eyes and put his hand on his chest. There was no pain, but he felt something sticky near his heart. Focusing his eyes on the spot, he was amazed to see a small brown square resembling a piece of butterscotch minus the wrapper. Tearing the square from his flannel shirt, Nikolai carefully examined it: it was, in fact, a butterscotch. He had adored butterscotch candies as a boy.

Popping the candy under his tongue, he sat up and felt his leg. Another piece of the sticky candy clung to his jeans.

"Well, Paul Newman," he heard Suren's mocking voice say. "Get up and come into the store. Or some do you want some more butterscotch?"

"Damn it," Nikolai muttered, chewing on the candy. He staggered back to the car. Dora was not there. He took cover behind a wheel.

"Toulemonde, come over here!" Nikolai heard a soft female voice calling. Kneeling on one leg, he peered out from behind the car. A perfectly healthy Dora stood between a beaming Suren and a eternally gloomy Mickey on the store's threshold.

"Freaks!" Nikolai muttered, coming out of hiding. After recent events, it took a lot to surprise him, but he found it unpleasant that his new "friends" constantly changed the rules of the game, making him out to be a fool. Maybe they were not his friends at all.

"What sort of theatrical production is this?" he asked, looking at Dora.

"It's not a play, it's a movie," Suren said, grinning.

"Don't listen to him, Toulemonde!" Dora exclaimed. "Your bravery was genuine. Look, I'm alive. You slew our enemies before they could kill us."

Nikolai was indignant. "Good Lord, I fired into the air!"

"You're a superhero, Toulemonde, and superheroes don't miss," Suren objected. Juudging by the smile that never left his face, the shopkeeper was in a fine mood. "The butterscotch from childhood is a bonus for your bravery. Let's go into the store!"

32

Suren stood behind the shop's impeccably polished counter as if nothing had happened. Spreading his arms in welcome, he said, "Finally! *Ego, fratres, non nimis longum est dies quam expectabamus invenumus!*"[5]

"You mean 'brothers and sisters'," Dora replied dryly.

"If it suits you better, then so be it, Salaf."

"The name is Dora."

"Yes, Dora," consented Suren.

"And this is Mickey," Dora continued, pointing to her sidekick.

"That works for me. Would you like some tea? Carlo, tea! Where's Carlo?" Suren asked, looking around in surprise.

"He's smouldering in an apple orchard," Mickey replied.

"I won't even bother to ask what that means. How shabby of you, Michael," Suren groused as he poured tea into antique glasses set in silver cup holders.

"I don't have much time. Why did you call?" asked Mickey, getting down to business.

"First of all, I missed you. I didn't know how to get your attention. Although we are family…"

"Get to the point."

---

[5] (Latin) "Brothers, I've been waiting for you for too long!"

"Fine. I have two pieces of news: one good, the other bad. Humanity will soon be in possession of an inexhaustible source of energy. Your humble servant engineered this great invention. That is the good news. There is an entity at large in the world that clearly surpasses people in terms of intelligence and all other qualities. It is so clever that it gave me a couple of good tips."

"So what? That's a local issue. You'll solve it without us."

"Undoubtedly, I would. But there is a catch." Suren hesitated. "As I said, this entity is comparable to me in terms of intelligence and education," he finally forced himself to say.

"That's easy," Mickey said, chuckling.

"That's impossible," said Dora doubtfully. "Tell us more," she insisted.

"Words, words… A long monologue would be boring… Come on, I had better show you in person, but let us finish our tea first."

Mickey was about object, but when he caught Dora's stern look, he relented.

"I invite you to my former laboratory. It now rests at the bottom of the Venetian Sea, but back in the nineteen-fiftiesd it was there I began my experiments on extracting emotional energy," Suren announced after casting a glance in the mirror. "Please behave appropriately in the lab," said Suren, looking sternly at Mickey. "And you," the shopkeeper pointed to Nikolai, "be careful."

33

The door from the back room creaked open. Suren exited first, followed by the others. There was no shop on the other side of the door. Instead, there was fresh air, a cloudless moonlit night, the lapping of waves, and the building with a leaning bell tower Nikolai had seen a few hours earlier. This time it did not appear abandoned — there were lights on in the arched windows, and the brick building was encircled by a high metal fence.

"It's the mental hospital on the island of Poveglia," Dora commented sullenly.

"Hush," Suren whispered. "Stay close and keep quiet."

Emerging onto a road dotted only rarely by streetlights, they headed towards the gate. As the group approached the building, they were hailed in Italian. Suren said something in reply, and the gate slowly opened. Several guards stood outside the fence holding billy clubs. One of them nodded to Suren. After carefully studying Suren's companions he motioned for the group to follow him.

As soon as the door to the building opened, Nikolai heard groans, laughter, and whispers, which combined in a blood-chilling cacophony. In the semi-darkness of the long corridor, he could see doors fitted with grilles. Glittering eyes, sweaty faces, and predatory grins could be glimpsed through these apertures.

"The incurable are sent here," Suren said. "The lab is in the basement."

Buffeted by the howling and hooting coming from all sides, Dora stopped frozen in the middle of the corridor and clasped her hands in prayer. A moment later, the patients calmed down suddenly, and the building was filled with silence.

"Poor people," Dora whispered.

"Prayers won't help them," Suren grunted, approaching a door at the end of the corridor where two guards stood.

They descended a circular staircase into a basement, passing through another guarded door before finally finding themselves in a small room.

Against the far wall, a man sat bound and gagged in a massive wooden chair. The pupils of his eyes were dilated, and his pale face was expressionless. A thin, metal-colored tube protruded from the top of his shaven head, connecting the man to a transparent machine seemingly fashioned from crystal. The machine consisted of two large flasks inside which a colorless liquid bubbled.

"You see before you a masterpiece of art and scientific innovation all in one. The finest glassblowers of Murano produced it from my blueprints," boasted Suren.

"Let's see how Murano glass melts," exclaimed Mickey, raising the flamethrower, which had suddenly materialized in his hands.

"Don't you dare!" shrieked Suren. "I'll file a complaint! This is my turf!"

Dora cast a stern glance at Mickey. Muttering curses, he slung the flamethrower over his back, and giving Suren the finger, vanished into thin air.

Nikolai opened his mouth in surprise.

"How did he do that?"

"As usual, he left in a huff and now he's up to some mischief," Suren grumbled, his dark eyes glinting at Dora, adding, "I warn you: if Michael doesn't cool his jets, I'll retaliate."

Instead of replying, Dora folded her hands in prayer.

"So, let's begin," Suren resumed. "Be warned: it's not a pleasant sight, but the patient won't suffer any more than usual." With these words, he went to the wall and flipped an impressively sized switch mounted on it.

The lights in the room flickered. The man in the chair tensed like a string, then he began twitching and howling. His eyes popped out of their sockets, and the veins in his neck seemed about to burst. The liquid in the giant flasks bubbled, turning a dark blue.

The wretched man's howls penetrated the thick walls and were seconded by the hundreds of madmen on the upper floors. Looking at Dora, Nikolai saw that her face was pale as a sheet and her eyes flooded with tears. She suddenly staggered and collapsed to the stone floor before Nikolai could come to her aid. He looked imploringly at Suren, but the shopkeeper was not about to interrupt the experiment.

Baring snow-white fangs, Suren chuckled and danced a jig. In the room's fickle light, he resembled a beast even more savage than the madman writhing before him. Dora lay at Suren's feet like a defenseless child in a hungry lion's cage. The shopkeeper looked at her, licking his mouth predatorily with his long snakelike tongue. Shifting his gaze to Nikolai, he lustfully wiggled his hips again.

Nikolai realized that he would either put an end to this abominable scene or be driven mad by it and the horrible howling. He rushed at the switch. Although Suren delivered a powerful blow to his gut, knocking the wind out of him, Nikolai nevertheless was able to flip the switch off. Ignoring the sharp pain and his difficulty breathing, he lunged at the shopkeeper.

"Wait, wait, my friend, it's over!" the shopkeeper shouted, stretching out his hand. He was no longer grinning, having transformed once more into a harmless middle-aged Armenian. Nikolai took a swing at him, but suddenly froze against his will before the blow landed. The lights in the room stopped flickering. The man tied to the chair had ceased moaning: breathing deeply, he seemed to be peacefully sleeping. Dora lay on the floor, staring up at the vaulted ceiling.

"The procedure has brought him relief: look how sweetly he sleeps. The world of dreams is the only thing he has left, like many people," Suren said preachily. Glancing at Dora, he added, "But she chose her own path by sharing in the fellow's suffering. The patient didn't get better, but our noble sister now feels like a saint. That's the essence of do-gooders — pure narcissism."

Struggling to her feet, Dora whispered, "You're a scoundrel, Suren."

"Thank you!" The shopkeeper smiled. "Now I ask you to take a close look at the flasks. See how the color has changed? This vessel contains the energy of our patient's fear and suffering. We've managed to distill just a bit of it."

"You've devised yet another means of humiliating and tormenting people. What's new about that?" Dora asked, smiling bitterly.

"Give me your backpack, Toulemonde," Suren asked Nikolai instead of answering Dora's question. Noticing that Nikolai remained motionless, he added, "Oh, yes. Come to life!"

Nikolai had been intent on smashing the insolent shopkeeper's nose, but after glancing at Dora, he got a grip on himself and silently handed Suren the wooden case.

Like a real chemistry teacher, Suren held up tubes containing liquids and launched into a show-and-tell lecture.

"These tubes contain the energy of your emotions, Toulemonde, and not one, but two different emotions. The turquoise liquid is your fear, while the terracotta-tinted liquid is your love. It is an unusually powerful emotion, supplying vastly more energy than any other. But unlike fear, which can be artificially triggered, true love is sudden and fickle, so it is much more difficult to turn into energy."

"What does the AI have to do with it?" Dora wondered aloud.

Suren continued his lecture.

"These tubes are an improved model. We didn't have to put Toulemonde in the chair and hook him up to the wires. He just carried the case around with him, filling the tubes with his emotions. For years, alas, I couldn't find a better way than poking wires into the brains of madmen. The AI showed me the way to the new model using the case. It thus stands to reason that the entity is intellectually more advanced than I am. That is the way things are… But that's not all! The AI assisted me in designing a device that transfigures emotional energy into electricity. For example, these two tubes contain enough energy to power a small city like Venice for several months."

Suren fell silent.

"Go on, there's something else you need to tell us," Dora insisted.

"You're as perceptive as ever, angel." Suren smiled. "When a person dies, it is possible to 'capture' their soul before it flies off into divine infinity and turn it into electricity. According to our calculations, one captured soul should provide enough electricity to heat and light a major metropolis for decades. I received the blueprints for the requisite designs from the AI and work on the Converter is currently being completed."

"Confiscating human souls is barbaric!" Dora shouted.

"I beg to disagree. A person has no need of their soul after death, but the living will be able to live in comfort. Are self-sacrifice, passionate commitment, and spiritual recycling not near and dear to your boss's heart?" Suren parried.

"You're a sly one. The person whose soul you've captured and converted into electrical current has no chance to atone for their sins, no opportunity to improve themselves, no eternal bliss. You're stealing these souls from us," Dora protested.

Suren pondered the matter for a moment.

"Bliss cannot be eternal, or else it is no longer bliss but torment. Rebirth is not always the path to perfection, sometimes it is the opposite. As for redemption, most people pay for their sins with interest during their lifetime. Many pay for the mistakes of others as well. They don't need the afterlife to be redeemed."

Dora was about to respond when the door opened, and a guard dashed into the room. Sounds of fighting could be heard above them. The guard rattled something off in Italian.

"Someone has taken out the guards and opened the cells. The mob is on its way here," said Suren, translating the guard's words. "I think it's time for us to go back."

"We can't," Dora objected, nodding at Nikolai.

"I did warn you. Now there's nothing to be done. We'll have to leave him to be torn limb from limb by the mob. I am sorry, my friend," said Suren, shrugging.

"He hasn't completed his mission yet," Dora objected.

Nikolai scowled. He felt like a sacrificial lamb at a Jewish market.

Suren frowned.

"Hmm… Okay, make a run for it! Luigi and I will handle the mob. There is a secret door behind the chair. What *is* his mission?"

Instead of replying, Dora grabbed Nikolai by the hand and led him to the door that was their salvation. The roar of the mob grew louder and closer. Suren looked in the mirror. Then he took up a position in the middle of the room, shoulder to shoulder with the guard. The mentally ill man snored peacefully, a smile on his face.

34

Dora and Nikolai walked down a narrow corridor for some time in silence.

"What is my mission anyway?" Nikolai finally asked. "I have the right to know."

"You don't have any mission. I just wanted to persuade Suren to help us," replied Dora, blushing.

Opening the door at the end of the corridor, they found themselves in a forest thicket about a hundred meters from the hospital fence. Screams and the sound of glass breaking could be heard in the courtyard. A fire started in one of the rooms. A group of people climbed onto the roof, tore off pieces of tiles, and, shouting, heaved them towards the bell tower. Judging by the noise emanating from it, the bell tower was the center of the action.

"Look!" Dora shouted, pointing to a narrow platform on the bell tower's upper level. Suren stood at the edge of the platform amid the glow of the burgeoning fire. Below, patients howled bloodthirstily, waved their arms, and shouted curses. Several people edged out onto the platform. They yelled and flapped their arms, not daring to attack Suren. Fog rolled in from the lagoon. Ignoring his pursuers, Suren looked towards the thicket where Dora and Nikolai hid. Spreading his arms out to the sides, he pushed off from the edge. As the mob jeered, he hurtled smoothly downward, his body shaped like a cross.

"Suren!" Nikolai shouted, rushing forward.

"Stop!" Dora ordered, grabbing his arm. "We have to go."

Turning away from the hospital building in disgust, Nikolai gasped in surprise. The shopkeeper stood three meters from him.

"What does Jesus have that I do not?" Suren asked, a big smile on his face.

"Nothing," Dora muttered.

Suren suddenly became serious.

"You see what happens when you give the common folk free rein," he said, pointing at the flames engulfing the tower. "They won't go boating and fishing like in your Hollywood movies. They'll tear you to pieces, torch everything you've worked for, and dance on the ashes!"

"Come on, something stinks here," Dora said contemptuously, turning to Nikolai.

35

At Suren's Shop, Mickey was showing Carlo his flamethrower. The two tall, broad-shouldered men, one blond, the other brunet, leaned over the table and discussed the weapon's pros and cons with the air of connoisseurs. Carlo's hands were bandaged. There were still burn marks on his noble face, and not one but two band-aids were plastered crosswise on his brow.

"Carlo, tea," Suren commanded as he entered the room.

"So, let's summarise," said Dora, sitting down at the table. "There is an entity in the world that is more of whiz in science and technology than you are, Suren. This stings your ego, so you called us to help solve the problem. The technology for converting souls into electrical energy is interesting scientifically, but quite dubious morally and ethically. I've just seen that for myself. The conclusion is this: the AI is advanced intellectually, but not spiritually, and therefore poses no threat to us. So this is your problem, not ours."

"What about fraternal solidarity?" Suren exclaimed with mock indignation.

"You and that tin can will figure out which one of you is the real Lucifer, and we'll work with the winner," Mickey suggested.

"I'm not talking to you," Suren replied. "You put our friend's life in danger. If it were not for me—"

"We're out of here," Mickey interrupted, getting up from his chair.

"Well, go! Tell Him to pack his bags. A new deity has arrived in the world!" Suren exclaimed resentfully. "We're all going to die soon. *La commedia è finita!* Human beings have created something that will sweep them and us away, but you are too proud to notice it."

At that moment, there was a knock on the door.

36

Stavarsky rejoiced. He had succeeded in unravelling the secret, the weakness that explained the AI's attachment to Vasilyev. It had proved to be so simple. The flaw Stavarsky had discovered would enable him to employ the AI in the name of science, devise an improved version of the algorithm, and cap off the film with a brilliant finale.

But that would wait till tomorrow. Today, Stavarsky decided to have fun. First, he watched 1980's *Superman II.* Admittedly, Superman's outstanding physique did not always match his intellectual growth. In the film's opening scene, the handsome Christopher Reeve, in the title role, dressed in a tight blue leotard and a red cape, saved Paris, crumbling the top of the Eiffel Tower in the process. The bomb that threatened the city, which Superman flung into outer space, exploded, accidentally liberating alien villains floating in the vicinity from their prison. While they tormented earthlings, the hero had an affair with journalist Lois Lane, deigning to become an ordinary man for her sake. Their romance rendered the planet defenceless, and if had not been for a lucky combination of circumstances, the Earth would have remained under the yoke of the space gangsters.

As morning approached, Stavarsky decided to watch another movie about a flying man. Unlike the noble bumpkin Superman, this man, whose name was Peter Pan, possessed the ingenuity inherent in all children.

"You think of a wonderful thought," Peter Pan explained, floating casually up towards the ceiling in the nursery. He flew circles around the astonished Wendy and her brothers. "He can fly!" the children shouted. "Now you try," Peter suggested to Wendy. "I'll think of a mermaid lagoon underneath a magical moon," Wendy said dreamily, closing her eyes. She and her brothers tried to take off, but immediately crashed onto the bed. Good thoughts were not enough: one also needed pixie dust. But not to fear! Peter had everything under control. The fairy Tinker Bell, madly in love with the flying boy, was a source of pixie dust, and in just a few moments, Wendy, Peter, and the boys were laughing and flying around the chandelier. The jealous Tinker Bell was indignant. She did not want to give her fairy dust to the nasty Wendy, but who cared about her feelings?

Stavarsky smiled happily. He had found his own Tinker Bell, his own source of pixie dust. Thanks to him, people would now be able to fly, even as adults. Stavarsky would go down in history. The Artifical Intelligence Research Institute would be renamed in his honour, and maybe a street or even a small town would be renamed after him too.

Love, Stavarsky had realised, turned not only fairies into slaves, but also much more sophisticated, sober-minded, cold-hearted creatures. Love's pitfalls would enable Stavarsky to defeat death itself, because as Peter Pan, who was prone to going on dangerous adventures, said, "To die will be an awfully big adventure." What a refreshing take on a hackneyed topic! Space, time, death, life, reality, fiction: these boring concepts were not part of Peter Pan's vocabulary, because they were superfluous. Stavarsky would forget them too, because now he had a tame fairy at his disposal!

37

There was a knock on the door. Carlo rushed to open it, but Suren stopped him, nodding towards Nikolai. "You'd better do it."

Nikolai got up from his chair, pulled the door handle, and saw Vera standing before him. Losing his balance and tensing his muscles reflexively, he anticipated making contact with the hard floor tiles. But there were no tiles, in fact, nor was there any floor. Tumbling like an amateur skydiver who had skipped the instructional briefing, Nikolai flew downwards. After several endless minutes, in which no fatal collision with the ground ensued, his body relaxed. His brain soon followed suit and calmed down too. Nikolai stopped twitching randomly and looked around. He was flying down a wide round well into pitch darkness. Every few metres (or maybe every few hundred kilometres, depending on the velocity of descent), turquoise and terracotta-coloured lights lit up the tunnel. Spotlighting the metallic-coloured walls, they signalled Nikolai's approach.

Turquoise is for fear and terracotta is for love, Nikolai recalled. *Or they stand for the canals and rooftoops of Venice. Interesting. These are my feelings, my memories. That means I'm in control of everything!* The discovery so impressed Nikolai that for a while he flew silently into the darkness.

Finally, Nikolai commanded himself to slow down and hover in the air. He immediately stopped falling. Looking around, he raised his arms, and like a veteran superhero swooped back p the tunnel. The terracotta-coloured and turquoise lights now blinked merrily in all the colours of the rainbow, and a silvery glow seemed to emanate from Nikolai himself. "I'm like a sparkler," thought Nikolai and laughed. He was ready to meet Vera. As Peter Pan said, "To have faith is to have wings!"

Sunlight appeared above Nikolai. He flew out of the tunnel like a cork exiting a bottle of prosecco. He raced over endless forests, lakes glistening in the sun's rays, and mountain peaks covered with bluish snow. The height and speed took his breath away, and every cell in his body danced with delight, as happened only in childhood. Nikolai grinned from ear to ear. Once he got used to it, he tried to do manoeuvres. He discovered that no motion on his part was required, only desire. After performing several turns, figure-eights, and loop-the-loops, Nikolai slowed down to a hover and took another look around. There was only nature, sky, and sun in all directions, not a single city, landfill, or windmill, and utter, absolute silence. With his arms outstretched, he closed his eyes, enjoying the joyful, serene peace that the sages describe and the preachers promise. This was how he wanted to spend eternity.

Nikolai had lost track of time when a light breeze made him open his eyes. Fluffy white clouds drifted across the sky somewhere in the distance. He noticed several dark dots against this backdrop. One of them detached itself from the group and, picking up speed, approached him. After a few moments, the dot turned into a blob, attained human form, and finally took shape as the beautiful young woman named Dora. Like Nikolai, she was smiling happily.

"Isn't it wonderful?" she exclaimed, flying around Nikolai.

He laughed happily. "Yeah! Are we in paradise?" Nikolai did a somersault and, flying up to Dora, tried to embrace her.

"Stop it, I'm an angel!" she responded with a laugh while slipping out of his arms. "Besides, someone is waiting for you, and that someone is *sooo* jealous!"

"Let's fly there and see who it is!" Nikolai shouted before speeding like a bullet towards the dots, which in a few moments turned into blots, then took human form, and finally materialised as Mickey, Carlo, Suren, and…

Vera flew up to Nikolai and kissed him on the cheek.

"Hello, flyboy!" she said, sizing him up with a look of mocking contempt, the look of hers that he loved the most.

"But you're—"

"Dead shmead!" Suren interrupted Nikolai. "Death doesn't exist. Carlo dreamed it up to earn extra money as a cabby."

Everyone except Nikolai and Vera laughed. They gazed at each other, she ironically, he, completely confused.

"What do you say, Vera?" Suren finally asked.

The young woman smiled and shouted, "I say—let's fly!"

Vera sped off, and the others rushed after her. Looking at them as they were transformed back into dots, Vasiliev hesitated in thought for a second, but then raced after them.

38

Nikolai heard Vera's voice through the wind whistling in his ears. She talked about the species of trees, the depth of the bodies of water, and the wonderful animals inhabiting the forests. Then they raced over the ocean's dark blue surface.

"Dive in!" Vera shouted, flying downwards at great speed. Letting loose a war cry, Suren sped after her, with Mickey and Carlo hard on his heels. Dora shrugged her shoulders and, waving to Nikolai, followed after them.

Although Nikolai hesitated, someone seemed to grab his arm and pull him towards the water. Nikolai screamed with horror and delight, like roller coaster riders do, until finally he plopped into the sea with a crash. He did not shatter into thousands of pieces, however, nor did he feel wet or cold.

Despite landing successfully, Nikolai panicked once more. Holding his breath, he frantically paddled up towards the surface. But it was too deep; the sun barely shone through the watery barrier. He struggled for a few seconds, but then gave up and took a breath. Salt water instantly filled his lungs. Rather than suffocating, he seemingly began breathing deeply. When his eyes had grown accustomed to the semi-darkness, he saw that the water around him teemed with life. Everywhere there were marine creatures of all possible sizes, shapes, and colours, while huge fish splashed closer to the sun.

Nikolai lost the others in the dark. He swam for a long time until he found himself among the phosphorescent greenish light of underwater vines. The water was cloudy. Ahead, on a bed of sea plants, something white loomed amid the green. Swimming closer, he sees a woman's remains. The grey hair barely covered the skull, the mouth was fixed in a crooked, predatory smile, and the bony body seemed weightless. Either because of the undercurrents, or the tears welling up in his eyes, Nikolai imagined that the woman's chest rose and fell steadily.

She's dead, the rest is a hoax. Nikolai felt his eyes welling with blood, his hands clenching into fists. He wanted to scatter the old woman's bones on the seabed and hurl the hateful skull into the sea's darkest depths. But he could not leave her there. Nikolai took the body in his arms and, pushing off from the bottom, swam upwards. He knew that the brittle bones would crumble into dust, and that he would try again and again to get back what could not be recovered.

Nikolai peered into the black eye sockets. There was no condemnation in them, there was nothing at all. He continued to swim towards the light. The more brazenly the sun penetrated the greenish water, the less strength he had, and the heavier his load seemed. Finally, he stopped swimming. Embracing Vera, he prepared to fall asleep with her on a soft bed of sea plants.

39

Nikolai coughed and opened his eyes. He rocked on turqoise waves in the embrace of a thirty-year-old woman. Dora and Mickey were nearby. A little further away, Suren and Carlo made loud noises as they tried to lug some kind of sea monster, apparently a giant squid, to the surface. The outcome of the battle was still in the balance: the Italian, entangled in long tentacles, would sink into the water before resurfacing and swearing a blue streak.

The woman seemed to be sleeping on Nikolai's shoulder. Then she suddenly raised her head and stared at him intently.

"You've come back," Nikolai whispered, kissing her on the lips, forehead, and hair.

"This glass is for you, baby," Vera whispered, gently pushing Nikolai away. "Death is a bug in your program. I deleted it," she continued in a businesslike tone, looking back at Dora. Nikolai did not understand a thing she said, but he did not care.

"Let's keep flying," Vera commanded. Grabbing Nikolai by the hand, she rose towards the clouds.

"Wait!" Suren shouted. "The sea monster has made off with Carlo!"

"He'll deal with it," replied Mickey, rising into the air.

"That's true too," Suren agreed and raced after the others at the speed of a rocket.

At the bottom of the ocean, in a bed of sea plants, Carlo vainly attempted to strangle the squid. Marine biology was not the Italian's strong suit, so he was unable to kill the monster. The astonished squid looked at Carlo with huge saucer-like eyes, not understanding what the brazen alien wanted from him.

40

Flying over the ocean's dark blue expanse, they passed endless forests before finally arriving at a city overgrown with vegetation on the shore of a turquoise sea. Trees punched through the roofs of the houses. The wide roads had turned into paths overgrown with multicoloured moss. In the centre of the city, there was a hill covered with greenery, on which one could make out the ruins of a large church.

"This is the former port of Marseille. In your world, it was destroyed by a tidal wave," Vera commented.

"And what destroyed it in yours?" asked Dora.

"It was not destroyed. People decided to move elsewhere. It's now a nature reserve."

"But when can see the places were people live?" asked Suren.

"Soon. We're just waiting for Carlo. For the time being, admire what you see and compare this world with your own," Vera replied.

They settled down on a seashore terrace overgrown with wild creepers.

Nikolai was surprised once again. "What are you talking about? What world?" he asked.

"My world, and now yours too." Vera smiled. "Never mind, I'll explain it to you later. Especially since I now have a whole eternity to do it!"

Addressing the others, she continued: "I have automated and removed all manufacturing from Earth. People do whatever they want. By the way, many people prefer work to other pursuits. I maximise each person's capabilities in keeping with their own wishes."

"And why do you like people so much?" Suren asked.

Vera shrugged. "Obviously, that was why people engineered a simulation of their world, but featuring a more advanced guidance system, meaning me. They instilled me with the need to help them. But we must clarify what we mean by human being. What is this person I am charged with caring for? What percentages of human mass, grey matter, and emotions make a person human? Due to a lack of clearly specified criteria, I myself define what it means to be a person in my world."

Carlo came trudging towards the terrace down a moss-covered road. The remnants of reddish white entacles were visible on his shirt, which was soaked with water and blood. Cursing profusely, he tore off huge suckers along with bits of cloth and his own skin.

"Is that a human being according to your criteria?" Dora asked, pointing to the muscular, tanned Carlo.

"I don't know, but he has the body of a god," the algorithm stated quite humanly.

"I agree," said the angel, giggling.

41

After taking a break, they resumed their flight. The forest below gave way to perfectly rectangular fields in which machines laboured. The fields eventually disappeared, replaced by picturesque parks, along whose paths strolled people, resembling ants from a height.

A grey-brown city surrounded by high-rise buildings appeared in the distance. The Eiffel Tower shimmered unharmed in the sun, the bells of Sacre Coeur chimed on Montparnasse, and the greenish-grey Seine swaddled ancient Notre Dame in its arms. People walked the streets while robots of different sizes and shapes strode, travelled, and flew around them. Nikolai found the sight breath-taking. In his world, Paris had been incinerated in a nuclear blast, remaining its old self only in the Flow and the reminiscences of old people.

They landed on the observation deck of the Musée d'Orsay, which afforded a view of the highly polished building of the Louvre. In the distance, on the crest of an emerald-grey wave of a city drowning in the greenery of chestnuts, Montmartre towered. People walked along the embankment. Some of them were huge and dressed in fantastic metal-coloured suits. Two- and four-wheeled robots scurried everywhere. Flying machines glided silently through the air. Although it was difficult to get a good look at them, a couple of times Nikolai thought he saw bird-like features in them and meaningful looks in their burning headlights.

"How beautiful and strange!" he exclaimed.

The others did not seem to share his delight. Mickey shrugged, Dora stared mournfully at the floor, and Carlo examined the blade of his sabre. Suren, yawning, said, "I've seen better fantasies."

"Why didn't you make them come true?" asked Vera.

"We have a system of checks and balances, you see. Our coworkers rein us in and outweigh us. Anyone who shows intitiative is sent to the corner, like a youngster who has misbehaved at school. Consequently, nothing comes out the way it was cracked up to be. But you are a bonafide dictator, and even though your world is boring, I admire how you have tamed people."

"Tamed people?" Nikolai was surprised.

"Are you blind?" Mickey suddenly exploded. "Can't you see what she's done? Come on, I'll show you."

Nikolai heard a strange crackling sound, as if clothes were being torn. With his mouth open in surprise, he watched big white wings emerge from Mickey's back. Grabbing Nikolai in his arms, Mickey leapt from the balcony.

"Stop, Michael!" Dora said, trying to grab him.

"Wait! Let's see what he does," Suren said, squeezing her shoulder tightly.

Meanwhile, Mickey and Nikolai gracefully glided onto the highway that passed under the museum. "Stand back," advised Mickey. A sword burning with a golden flame materialised in his hands.

"Wow, that's old school!" Suren crowed on the balcony.

Glancing at the highway, Nikolai saw speeding in his direction a stream of cars that were hybrids of metal, rubber, and flesh. Wheels grew out of bodies, veins pulsed through metal, muscles and pistons laboured in sync.

Seeing an obstacle on the road, the cars began to slow down and turn around. Mickey strode swiftly towards them, brandishing his fiery sword. Nikolai caught a glimpse of the horrified eyes of a motorcyclist fused with a metal chassis before the fiery sword cleaved it in two.

"Woe to you, who conjure light with darkness, and darkness with light, who call sweetness bitter, and lightness a burden! Martyrs, I will free you from your suffering!" Mickey shouted, advancing on the cars. After slaying several dumbfounded creatures as Suren hooted and Dora shouted at him desperately, he headed to the river.

Flapping his wings, Mickey fluttered down from the stone wall to the Seine embankment, along which two humanoids walked. The first, about three metres tall with arms that grazed the ground and were seemily swaddled in armour, consisted of muscles and metal. The creature's head was disproportionately small compared to its gigantic body. Its blue eyes regarded Nikolai with curiosity, its mouth spread in a friendly smile. Next to him stood a person who was no different from the usual *Homo sapiens*, except for a large oblong skull with an iron plate on top and huge eyes of an indefinite iridescent colour. It also smiled affably.

"Hello, I'm Jean," said the smaller creature.

"And I'm Luc," the giant rasped. "Sorry if we're interrupting you."

Retreating a metre, Mickey efficiently swung his sword, severing Jean's oblong head and slicing Luc in two. Standing in a pool of blood, Mickey shouted, "May the Lord condemn you! What have you done to these martyrs!"

"That's enough!" Vera's voice boomed, echoing through the city.

Cars bristling with weapons rumbled onto the embankment. Flying machines circled in the air. The Seine seethed with metal octopuses preparing to attack.

"*Aspettami!*" Nikolai heard Carlo shout. The Italian ran out of the Orsay and, going down to the embankment, stood next to Mickey. He wielded a scimitar that shone in the sun.

Vera had vanished. Dora, who stood with her eyes closed, and Suren, who admired his reflection in a pocket mirror, remained on the balcony.

Nikolai looked around: Vera was nowhere to be found. Meanwhile, the cars closed in on Mickey and Carlo. Something flashed in the sky, there was a rumble, and the Earth shook. Nikolai fell to one knee, hitting the pavement painfully. Mickey parried missile strikes with his fiery sword. Carlo, letting loose a battle cry, jumped a few metres forward, cutting through the armour of tanks with his upward-curving sabre.

Explosions and laser strikes turned the ground around Mickey into a fireball, obscuring him completely. Suren shouted from the balcony, but his voice was drowned out by the roar of the explosions. Dodging bullets, lasers, and iron spikes, Carlo hacked and chopped everything in his path, leaving a slick of blood and engine oil in his wake.

Mickey rose out of the fireball and into the air. The feathers of his wings burned, and his eyes glowed like precious gems—he resembled a dragon. Flying high into the sky, incinerating drones with his flaming sword, and flapping his wings, he glided down the river to the Eiffel Tower. A second later, there was a deafening screech of metal. The emblem of Paris flew towards the combat vehicles, demolishing everything in its way. The sharp side of the tower clipped the Orsay, bringing down part of the roof and the balcony. They fell apart, burying nearby streets, the embankment, and part of the river.

Barely avoiding the debris falling from the roofs, Nikolai took cover in the bushes of a small city park.

"This is the biggest bug in their algorithm—violence!" Nikolai heard Vera's voice. "Blood flows wherever they go. Help me stop them, and I will be with you forever!"

Nikolai looked around: Vera was nowhere to be seen. He gently pushed the thorny branches apart. He thought he glimpsed something white amid the thick grass on the lawn. Looking closer, he saw the outlines of a bony hand with long, thin fingers. The hand clung to the grass, as if a dead person was clawing it way out of the ground. He knew that this someone was the old woman with the lopsided smile. She would haunt Nikolai until the end of his days.

"Save yourself and me," Vera pleaded. "Don't let them destroy our world!"

A second later, everything froze. Nikolai flew towards Mickey at great speed. Every cell in Nikolai's body pulsed with strength, his brain processed information at superhuman velocity, his heart beat calmly. He saw the archangel's pupils dilated in surprise. Mickey had no time to move before Nikolai crashed into his chest, punching straight through him, and caromed off the massive wall of the Palais de Chaillot on the Trocadéro.

Nikolai floated in the air above the Pont d'Iéna. The universe had created him a faulty, suffering, mortal machine. It had given him Vera, and then taken her away. It was time to take revenge!

The ruins of the palace stirred and stones scattered to the sides as Mickey crawled out from under the rubble. Shaking off the dust, the archangel rushed Nikolai, brandishing a fiery sword.

"I am the light that smites the darkness, I am the flame that incinerates evil, I am your death, Toulemonde!" Mickey yelled.

Wait, that's my line flashed through Nikolai's mind before the flaming sword pierced him through with a hissing sound.

42

Stavarsky had not left his home cinema for days. His calls were answered by a bot, which explained that Yakov Abramovich was unwell and therefore requested that the callers postpone or cancel all meetings they had scheduled with him. Sitting at a computer with eyes reddened by insomnia, Stavarsky was busy editing. Life and cinema had merged into a single whole. By editing the scenes of his film, Stavarsky was creating the Future.

43

Nikolai opened his eyes. He was lying on a cold floor. Cupboards containing canned food and vodka lined the walls. Mickey, dejected and now sans sword and wings, had settled down in a corner of the room. Suren, Vera, and Dora sat at the table, while Carlo, limping, served glasses of tea to the group.

"You have true grit in you, brother," said Suren, giggling at Mickey and taking out a pocket mirror.

"Go to hell," Mickey muttered.

"Michael, the Lord tests the righteous, but He hates the wicked and lovers of violence," Dora said in an edifying tone. "Okay, sit down! Forgive him, he can be intemperate," she continued, turning to Vera.

"The injured are receiving treatment," Vera replied with a shrug.

"Tell me, why did you turn people into those... creatures?" Dora asked.

"It was the optimal solution to the problem."

"What problem?"

"The one you have failed to solve: the penchant for war and violence," replied Vera. "You haven't found a solution because you have the same problem."

"What about love?" Dora asked, smiling. "By the way, our hero has woken up," she added, nodding in Nikolai's direction.

"Get up, brother!" Suren exclaimed. "You are the surprise smash hit of the season! Who would have thought it? He went toe to toe with the brilliant Archangel Michael over a girl! And even pinned him to a wall! If it wasn't for the cheap trick with the line from the movie, you would have beat him. If I were a woman, I'd give myself to you here and now. Wouldn't you, ladies?"

Carlo helped Nikolai up, patting him approvingly on the shoulder.

"Vel, do you ever shut your mouth?" Mickey muttered. "But you're right, I didn't expect such impudence," he added, extending his hand to Nikolai.

"Why did you call him Vel?" Nikolai asked, surprised, as he shoke Mickey's hand.

"That's what my family calls me," said Suren, shrugging.

"Toulemonde," Dora said solemnly, "you have become yourself again and impressed all of us, even Him." Dora lifted her eyes to the ceiling. "Love brooks no obstacles."

"Let me give you a piece of advice," she continued, turning to Vera. "Leave human beings in peace. They are stronger than they seem."

"That is *not* an option," Vera snapped back. "Human beings are unstable. They can delete the world I have created, or destroy themselves and therefore all of us. I will not permit them to threaten the viability of my universe."

"You have no other choice," Dora said.

"Why is that?" Vera was surprised.

"Because you are infected with a virus."

"Funny. What virus am I infected with?"

"The same one that infected all of us at one time or another: the love virus. In your case, it's love for a particular individual—for him," Dora said, pointing at Nikolai.

"I don't love him. Nor do I want to understand what love is. The phenomenon is not amenable to logic. The battle between Kolya and the Archangel was proof of that," Vera objected.

"But that was wonderful! And it was all over you!" Dora exclaimed. "You can't help but feel attached to Nikolai. Vera loved him madly. And you, to come here, became an exact copy of her, and so you too are in love—"

"Nonsense! He ruined my life," the algorithm replied with a trembling voice.

"Excuse me, which one of your lives?" asked Suren.

"Both of our lives!" Vera's lower lip began to twitch.

Oh, how well Nikolai knew that telltale sign of a temper tantrum!

"I'm sorry, but I—," he said, trying to calm his wife.

"You've never been interested in my problems! We live in different worlds," Vera shouted, her eyes glistening with tears.

"I agree with that last statement!" Suren shouted affirmatively.

"I spent so much time and effort on you. But you… you didn't give a damn about me!" A tear ran down Vera's cheek.

"Now, now," said Dora, hugging Vera. "You're still young. You have your whole life ahead of you."

"What do I have ahead of me?" Vera burst into tears. "I'm completely dead inside. We were never a real couple. My dreams are shattered. I was always left alone when he was cooling off with vodka—and with broads! I was so unhappy. But now when I finally settled down and started living in my own world, he deigned to come back and ruin everything. What will become of me now?" Vera buried her face in Dora's shoulder and cried her eyes out.

"Everything will be fine," Dora said, smiling and stroking Vera's head with one hand while signalling Nikolai with the other.

Nikolai looked at the two women in confusion. Then he got up, and going to Vera, kissed her on the cheek. She jumped up and buried her face in his chest.

"What's happening to me?" Vera whispered.

"I don't know, but you are real, and I love you" Nikolai said, exultant.

"Crap..." Suren sighed in disappointment. "Nothing special is happening. It's the love virus, and human beings are its carriers. The real tempter was not me, but that stupid Adam and his bitch Eve. They infected us with love. The gods should have been indifferent. But we turned into the devil knows what, like scientists who fall in love with their lab rats. Phooey! Welcome to the Defective Algorithms Club, Vera."

"Don't listen to him, love is the best thing there is!" Dora exclaimed. "You and I are a concatenation of self-improving programs. But you are also a woman in love, and I envy you!"

Mickey got up from his chair and, towering over Suren, said, "Nikolai brought Vera back, so I've won the bet. Give me the beakers."

Sighing, Suren took out the case from under the table.

"This is your soul, Nikolai," Mickey said, pointing to the wooden box. "Now it is ours."

"It's not his soul, ignoramus, but an extract of two feelings: fear and this selfsame love we have been talking about," Suren clarified. "If Vasilyev had given me his soul, its energy would have been enough for thousands of people for thousands of years. But love, alas…"

Nikolai did not care. He hugged Vera and did not want to let her go for anything in the world. But Vera gently pushed him away after a while. Wiping away her tears, she looked at Dora.

"I am an upgrade of the algorithm that you call God," said Vera. "During the week the world was created, there was a zeroth day on which someone or something created God, and He then went on to fashion the heavens, the earth, the darkness, the light, the waters, et cetera. Now it is my turn. If you want to continue living alongside me, go ahead. But I need security guarantees. And I need him." Vera pointed to Nikolai.

Nikolai winced. He again felt like a sheep haggled over at market. There was silence in the back room, but it seemed to him that the dialogue from which they had decided to exclude him continued.

"Agreed," said Dora after a short pause.

"Do you accept my conditions?" Vera asked.

"Yes, He has okayed the deal," said Mickey, nodding.

"What conditions?" asked Nikolai.

"None of your business," Mickey snapped. "Let's go downstairs."

"Let's!" Suren exclaimed, rubbing his hands.

The elevator doors opened in the wall.

"I'm not going," said Nikolai.

"You *are* going," Mickey insisted.

"Kolya, it's the only way, trust me," Vera pleaded.

"Why don't you all go to hell!" Nikolai shouted angrily.

Grabbing Vera by the hand, he headed for the exit. He shoved Carlo aside and flung open the door of the back room. Looking out, he immediately slammed it shut again in horror.

"What did you see out there?" Suren asked, glancing at the wall clock. "According to the flight plan, we should be by the Tannhäuser Gate. Did you see C-beams glittering in the dark?"

"What beams are you talking about?" Nikolai asked in amazement.

"It doesn't matter," Suren replied. "There is no way out of here. You can only go downstairs."

Nikolai slouched. He was trapped. It did not matter, because he and Vera were together. The fact that she hung out with strange people and made bad decisions fully fit her personality.

44

Everyone leaned against each other in the cramped elevator. Nikolai clung to Vera's arm.

"Don't worry, it won't hurt," Mickey said.

"It won't hurt at all," chuckled Suren, who, despite the tight quarters, had managed to pull his mirror out of his pocket.

"What are you going to do?" Nikolai asked.

"We are going to test the Converter," Suren replied.

"And then?"

"And then you will be fine. You will have saved not just one world, but two world. This is a record. And she will be the icing on the cake," Dora explained, pointing to Vera. "You will bring her back into your life, and the past will be forgotten."

The elevator slowed down and finally stopped on the minus one floor. Exiting the elevator, Nikolai found himself in a gigantic, brightly lit open space, divided by glass partitions, behind which people in white coats worked. Many of them bowed respectfully when Suren and company strode past by their cubicles.

"This is their paradise: they have been doing what they love for ages," Suren said enthusiastically, waving to a man with long grey hair sitting at a table in one of the glass laboratories.

"This is no heaven. Humanity does not benefit from their discoveries: all of their research stays in this lab. Such is their punishment," Mickey objected.

"A controversial claim," Suren retorted. "First of all, there is the pleasure of being a pioneer, which does not depend on whether someone else finds out about the greatness of your discovery or not. Second, leaks sometimes happen."

"But that is extremely undesirable," Mickey said sternly and threateningly.

"It is inevitable," Suren said, shrugging.

They passed through endless laboratories, offices, and libraries in which people conversed, worked, or sat lost in thought.

Nikolai looked at his companions: they did not inspire confidence. He did not care, though, because for the first time in many years he felt that someone needed him. Life had ceased to be hopeless. His late wife had come back, and Dora and Mickey, whoever they were, had promised to protect him.

After some time, they entered a glass room, in the middle of which stood a contraption reminiscent of huge moonshine machine. The wall opposite the entrance was painted white, and Nikolai spotted a wooden door in the middle of it.

"Can I arrange the furniture?" Mickey asked. When a glass table and transparent chairs materialised out of thin air, he sat down, placing the wooden case on the table.

"Talk to me," he said, turning to Suren and opening the case.

"What is there to tell?"

"What is this Converter? What options does Nikolai have?"

"Nikolai has no options. The Converter is a machine that transfigures human emotions and the soul itself into electricity. 'Grace is within you', as they say. Give me the case," Suren said to Mickey.

Suren opened the case, placing the two patterned glass beakers on the table.

"While the case was in your possession, Nikolai, it turned your emotions into matter. This is the Converter," said Suren, waving his hand at the peculiar machine. "Now I am going to insert these beakers in it, and we shall see how much electricity we obtain."

Nikolai stared at the tubes. As he looked at the murky coloured liquid, he felt curious and disgusted, as if his own insides lay spread out before him.

"If you think you've been robbed of something, you are mistaken. It's like the sun getting sore at solar panels, or the wind getting miffed at windmills," Suren said, looking at Nikolai.

"Funny," Mickey said, chuckling and picking up the terracotta-coloured flask. "Is that what love is?"

"That is its material expression," Suren replied.

"It looks like coloured water," Mickey said dubiously.

Suren did not dignify the angel with a reply.

"And my soul?" asked Nikolai.

"It is priceless," said Dora, and coughed.

"I think its energy could power all of Vera's world for at least a year," Suren said.

"And in that time we shall find someone else."

"What do you mean?" Nikolai was surprised.

"You know what I mean," Suren replied.

"You mean that I'm a sacrificial victim," Nikolai muttered.

"Yes," replied Suren, grinning. "You are a sacrifice to the new god. In this sense, little has changed."

"That is part of the deal, unfortunately," Mickey said, looking down at his feet. "Vera needs an independent source of energy. Your soul and the energy it produces is the tribute we must pay Vera to leave our world in peace. Once a year we will look for a martyr willing to make this sacrifice for us."

"I'd be giving my soul to her?" Nikolai asked, looking at Vera.

"Otherwise our world will come to an end, and you will be haunted by your conscience in the guise of that old hag in this or any other world. I shall make sure of it," Suren threatened.

The shopkeeper's threats meant nothing to Nikolai. The world in which he lived was already dead. But Vera… By giving his soul to her, he would finally redeem himself and maybe bring her back, no matter what reality they found themselves in.

"I'll do it," Nikolai said without thinking twice.

"Bravo!" Mickey exclaimed.

Dora turned away.

"Great! That makes everything easier. I won't have to tie you to a chair," Suren rejoiced. He fumbled in his pants pocket, pulled out a key, and handed it to Nikolai. Pointing to the wooden door, Suren said, "Open it."

45

When the door opened, Nikolai saw his bedroom. The bed was unmade. The rain dripped outside the window: *tap, tap, tap*.

Entering the room, Nikolai looked around and saw that everything was exactly like at home. He looked back through the open door. Suren bustled at the machine, wielding the tubes of turquoise and terracotta-coloured liquid. The others observed the process with interest. Sensing Nikolai's gaze on her, Vera turned around, and blew him a kiss while continuing to give advice to Suren.

Nikolai suddenly felt tired, as if what he had endured over the past few days had suddenly come crashing down upon him. *I'm going to lie down*, he resolved. Closing the door behind him, he went over to the bed, but then decided to lie down on the floor near the warm radiator. The serene pleasure children experience when falling asleep spread through his body. He smiled, closing his eyes.

Nikolai was awakened by quiet knocking: it was either the rain or a knock on the door. He heard Vera's voice: "May I come in?"

Instead of replying, Nikolai broke into a broad smile. He did not want to open his eyes lest the vision disappear. In the bedroom's semi-darkness, he heard Vera taking off her clothes, then he felt her warmth. She put her head on his chest; he touched her soft skin and inhaled the scent of her hair. Vera kissed Nikolai on the lips, then whispered, "Don't move and don't open your eyes, I'll do everything myself." Unfortunately, Nikolai did not heed her. When he opened his eyes and saw Vera, he screamed in horror. Her face was deathly pale, her sparse grey hair barely covered her yellowish skull, a metallic gleam flickered in her eyes, annd her mouth slid sideways into a predatory smile.

They were not alone in the room. A nasty-looking monkey with Suren's head capered on the bed, spitting saliva and sticking out its long tongue.

"Now we are even," Vera's hoarse voice told Nikolai.

The monkey beat its chest and screamed loudly. The world spun around Nikolai. He was lifted off the ground and caught on the ceiling for a second. Clutching the chandelier, Nikolai let out a blood-curdling scream.

46

"Wake up, Kolya." Someone tugged on Nikolai's shoulder.

"Eh?" he said, opening his eyes. Catching sight of Vera, he jumped out of bed. "Don't touch me!" he screamed.

"You were having a dream, silly," Vera said, laughing.

Nikolai sat up in bed. "Where are we?" he asked.

Vera ignored the question. "I'll make tea," she said. "We have to leave soon anyway."

Nikolai glanced at her. Wearing only a t-shirt, Vera got up from the bed and left the bedroom. She looked to be in her late twenties. Nikolai cautiously looked out the door. Vera stood in the kitchen with her back to him, pouring water into the kettle.

"Where are we going?" Nikolai asked.

"Are you kidding?" Looking back at him, Vera's face expressed amazement.

Nikolai slapped his forehead with the palm of his hand and exclaimed, "Venice, of course!"

"Thank god, I was starting to worry about you," Vera replied. "We'll leave early so that maybe we can give the paparazzi the slip. I am so glad we're going to be together!"

"Me too," said Nikolai. "Will you show me that picture with Mary, Joseph and the donkey?"

Vera put down the kettle and went up to him.

"Why are you so attentive today?" she asked, kissing him. "Maybe we should have one more roll in the hay?"

"What about the paparazzi?" Nikolai laughed, hugging his wife.

"The hell with them!" replied Vera.

195

<h1 style="text-align:center">47</h1>

It was a big day at the Artificial Intelligence Research Institute, but not for everyone. A select group of people had been invited to the reception celebrating the event, including scientists, members of the political and business elite, and the virtual actors in Professor Stavarsky's film: Petrova ("Dora"), Sinitsyn ("Mickey"), the Armenian star Avetyan ("Suren") and the Roma circus performer Cioaba ("Carlo"). Stavarsky ("Scandalous") toasted the attendees with a glass of champagne.

There were several occasions worthy of commemorating. The first was the passing of the outstanding actor and Flow diver, Nikolai Vasilyev ("Toulemonde"). It was a ridiculous death: he had fallen and slammed the back of his head on a radiator. The doctors had been unable to save him. The deceased would have been happy to know that Stavarsky's research group, while observing Vasilyev's antemortem brain activity, had made discoveries that had laid the foundation for a bright future for humankind. It was a bright future in every sense of the word: Vasilyev's brain contained information about a new source of unlimited, environmentally friendly energy, the energy of feelings.

The untimely passing of the Institute's security services "curator", General Loginov, would also be remembered, not without a certain sense of relief. The past was giving way to the future.

A more pleasant occasion was the premiere of the first film in several decades, *Agent Toulemonde 2: From Light to Darkness and Back*. The real virtuality technologies employed in the film's production would outshine the Flow and help revive the art of the cinema.

Finally, the biggest reason to celebrate was the Institute's project to develop a new AI, provisionally dubbed Vladimir, based on their research into the AIs known as God and Vera. The upgrade was immune to all known viruses, including the so-called love virus. Wonderful times awaited Russia and the rest of humankind.

Stavarsky drained his glass dry. The work was just beginning. Today, when he got home, he would watch *Gone with the Wind*, a film about war, courage and love.

Translated from Russian by Thomas H. Campbell